ATLANTIS ATTACKS

Revenge of the Hollow Earth

David Johnson

Published by New Generation Publishing in 2015

Copyright © David Johnson 2015

First Edition

The author asserts the moral right under the Copyright, Designs and Patents Act 1988 to be identified as the author of this work.

All Rights reserved. No part of this publication may be reproduced, stored in a retrieval system or transmitted, in any form or by any means without the prior consent of the author, nor be otherwise circulated in any form of binding or cover other than that which it is published and without a similar condition being imposed on the subsequent purchaser.

ISBN: 978-1-78507-698-5

Cover design by Jacqueline Abromeit
Cover art by Ian Rose and David Johnson

www.newgeneration-publishing.com

New Generation Publishing

About the author

David Johnson lives in Wiltshire, UK, with his family and friends. His love of travel, history, Sci-Fi, films and current affairs has all contributed to this story. His fascination with local places like Stonehenge, Avebury, and neighbouring Glastonbury has been central to establishing key elements of the story

He uses local places he knows, overseas places he has visited and historic events he is interested in to blend into this fast-paced young adults Sci-Fi quest. He has also been a guest speaker at International writing events abroad and at schools in the UK, New Zealand and Eire.

David helps raise funds for charity through Sci-Fi group events for children.

Also available by David Johnson

Crystal Quest books 1-5
Part 1: Time Trap ISBN 978-1-905203-31-4
Part 2: Fires of Fury ISBN 978-1-905621-51-4
Part 3: Destiny and Destruction ISBN 978-1-906206-49-9
Part 4: Atlantis Betrayed ISBN 978-1-906710-39-2
Part 5: Dark Victory ISBN 978-1-907499-27-2

Battle for Atlantis ISBN13: 978-1-78003-146-0

Chapter One

The flying saucer emerged from its faster-than-light space vortex and slowed dramatically as it approached the Earth.

Undetected by humans, it swiftly entered a high orbit and positioned itself over Western Europe. Next it began a controlled descent over the British Isles; cutting its way through the atmosphere like a shooting star.

The air around it still burned bright red as it emerged from the clouds; then the glow faded as it suddenly slowed and levelled off. Safely through the atmosphere it instantly stopped and floated motionless for a few moments. Then as quickly as it had stopped, it silently sped off horizontally as if the laws of gravity did not apply to it.

Skimming over rooftops and between hills it moved so fast it was like a blur, travelling unseen in the early morning light.

*

Anne Cristal sliced her way through the water of the swimming pool as fast as she could. Despite years of practice and good quality goggles, the chlorine still stung her eyes. At sixteen she was her school's best swimmer and this early morning practice session was essential to maintaining her fitness and chances of winning the regional championships.

Today she was the only swimmer in the town's public swimming pool, as her pre-school training gave her the unhindered opportunity to practice as much as she could. Her front crawl was her best discipline and she had worked hard to perfect her timed breathing to a high standard. If she wanted to win, she had to practise.

Suddenly her vision blurred and her entire body felt as if it had suffered an electric shock. For a moment she thought that she was going to drown as her limbs tingled and went numb. Then everything around her turned bright white and she vanished from the water. For a fraction of a second the place where she had been left a hole the exact shape of her body. Then the water poured into the void and it was as if she had never been there. A moment later the white light faded and she found herself slumped on the floor of a person-sized glass tube. She was still in her black one-piece swim suit and tiny bobbles of chlorine water still clung to it, dripping onto the floor of the tube. Anne was tall, slim and athletic looking. She had straight shoulder length blonde hair and smooth pale skin. Suddenly she became aware that her mind was whirling, filling with pointless random thoughts. She knew that she needed to clear her head and had to snap herself out of the shock of being sucked out of the water. Slapping herself hard across the right cheek did the trick.

As soon as she cleared her mind, she sprang to her feet and hit the glass as hard as she could with both fists, hoping to push open a concealed hatch or break it. Unfortunately the transparent material did not budge or crack.

Taking a few deep breaths to calm herself, she slicked back her long blonde wet hair from her face then pulled off her swimming goggles. Squinting, she looked beyond the glass barrier of the tube to see into the room beyond. She immediately gasped as she saw the room was circular, about sixty feet in diameter with metallic walls. The floor and ceiling were also made of shiny metal. Spaced around the walls at regular points were dozens of glass tubes, just like the one she was trapped inside. In the centre of the room was a circular metal table, with strange flashing instruments and plastic bottles fitted on top. The room was lit by white glowing orbs the size of dinner plates set into the ceiling.

Where was she? How did she get here? Who had brought her here?

As if in answer a round door opened in the opposite wall and a weird object floated in. It was a glass and metal tube the size and shape of an old-fashioned dust bin. On top of it was a translucent red glass dome. Silently the object floated across to the tube where Anne was imprisoned, stopped and hovered.

Then through the circular door strode two human looking figures. One, obviously the leader by his confident gait, walked ahead of the other. He wore a strange one-piece silver metallic space suit with matching boots and belt. He was tall and thin, with chalk white skin and a narrow band of jet black hair running from between his eyebrows over the top of his head to the back of his neck. However, what unnerved Anne the most was his all-white eyes, with tiny pin-prick pupils.

The other man was very short, a little over four feet tall. He had a bulging stomach and large swollen head with round green eyes. Recoiling in horror, Anne thought that his weird toothy grin was evil rather than friendly.

He wore a metallic outfit, over which he wore what looked like a surgeon's apron. On his head he had a surgeon's headpiece consisting of a small positional light, magnifying eye lenses and a radio ear piece.

The tall man finally spoke with a deep commanding voice. "I am Prince Cronus, commander of this craft. This is Hades my master scientist and the hovering robot is my medical flyer called Seth. We have kidnapped you for your special genetic heritage. Seth will now take a sample from you."

Despite her rising tide of fear, Anne recognised the names as myths of Greek and Egyptian origin. Cronus was the Greek God of death and destruction, Hades the Greek God of the underworld and Seth the Egyptian God of chaos and death.

The hovering robot suddenly extended a twisting telescopic metal tentacle out of its body and pointed it at the glass tube containing Anne. The flat end then opened like six metal petals and a long needle extended from it. Anne recoiled in horror as the needle touched the glass and passed through it without breaking it.

Desperate to escape it, she pressed herself back against the tube, but the needle got longer and moved sideways towards her. Shouting defiance she turned her head and looked away as the needle pricked her arm and began its work.

Chapter Two

Lucy Cristal had gone to the local public library while her sister Anne had gone to the swimming pool. It was the one day of the week when it opened especially early in the morning and she was keen to do some extra study. While her sister was extrovert and sporty, fourteen-year-old Lucy was quiet and thoughtful. She also differed in other ways; brunette rather than blonde, thin rather than athletic, and a few inches shorter. She wore a long black skirt and knee high black boots, a rainbow coloured baggie pullover and her long dark hair was tied back in two plaits.

Lucy sat at a round table in the far corner of the library, behind a solid book case out of everyone's sight. She was bent over a pile of books and busily transferring the information she needed into her school folder. Despite being the brains of the family she preferred to browse through books rather than the internet. The librarian and her assistant were at the far side of the building carrying out admin tasks. As Lucy was a trusted, regular pupil, they left her to get on with her studies unsupervised.

Suddenly a blinding white light surrounded Lucy, causing her vision to blur and her body to feel as if it was suffering an electric shock. She tried to shout for help but instead felt the air being sucked out of her lungs. And then in the blink of an eye she vanished from the library. A moment later she appeared in a person-sized transparent tube, inside a large circular metal room. She screamed loudly and hit the tube with both clenched fists, but her hands merely bounced off the unbreakable material.

Barely holding back her sobs she slid slowly to the floor of the tube and sat with her back against its inside, facing into the centre of the room. She suddenly felt scared and cold, so she drew her legs up under her baggy jumper. The rising tide of fear in her grew as she saw that the wall of the room was lined with tubes identical to the one she was trapped in. Her fears grew ever greater as she saw on the far side there were three figures. Trembling, she folded her arms around her chest hoping to find comfort in the warmth of her rainbow coloured baggie pullover. Then suddenly, more in frustration than hope, she kicked at the tube with both feet, but as she suspected, her boots had no effect and the transparent material did not break.

In response to the noise, one of the figures turned to look at her, next the other shapes moved away from the tube in front of them and Lucy saw who was in the tube. It was her older sister Anne!

Lucy leapt to feet again at the sight of her and began banging frantically on the glass. But her sister just sat in her tube looking dazed, unable to recognize her. Now that the two weird men and the floating robot had finished with Anne, they turned and began to move across the room towards Lucy.

Once again Lucy screamed at the top of her voice.

*

George Cristal sat by himself in a quiet corner of the school's playground. He had got there early and alone, as both his sisters had other better things to do; Anne her swimming and Lucy her studying. He normally got ordered out of the house by his mum at the same time his sisters left, so if he was not meeting his friends, he usually cycled to school straight away to have maximum time to play games on his hand held computer. Ten year old George had shoulder length wavy blond hair and was tall for his age. He had distinctive piercing blue eyes, square jaw and already a well developed rebellious streak. Not a trouble-maker, but someone who challenged the way things were. Unlike his sisters he was very technology orientated and had already begun to develop his own computer games.

He sat on the concrete ground with his back against the wall of the main school hall, tucked away behind some bushes where he would not be disturbed until the bulk of his friends arrived.

Suddenly he was aware of a shadow falling over him. Annoyed, he looked up expecting to see a teacher standing over him. Instead he was shocked to see a large flying saucer hovering silently in the sky above him. It was dull grey and over a hundred feet in diameter.

Mouth open with astonishment he found he couldn't take his eyes off it. As if hypnotised he was forced to slowly stand up causing his game machine to drop from his fingers. Even as it hit the floor and broke open, he found himself unable to call out.

Then the saucer descended closer to him and his hair began to stand on end, as if he was experiencing an electric shock. He tried to call for help again but nothing came out of his gaping mouth. Instead he was suddenly bathed in a glowing white light so intense it forced him to close his eyes to block out the brightness. The next moment he vanished from the school and reappeared inside the flying saucer. Opening his eyes he saw that he was in a transparent tube set into the wall of a large circular room.

Having an interest in computers and science fiction he instantly guessed that he had been beamed up into the flying saucer. As soon as his head cleared of its confusion he realised that there were two weird humanoid figures and a floating robot in the centre of the room. They were poised as if waiting for him to arrive. Desperate to find a way out he looked around the room until he suddenly saw that his sisters were slumped unconscious in their own tubes.

"We were expecting you George," said the leading alien, his tiny pin-prick pupils fixing George with a hypnotic trance. The boy was shocked to see that the man had chalk white skin and a narrow band of jet black hair running from between his eyebrows over the top of his head to the back of his neck. The other man was a little over a meter tall and had an extended stomach and a larger than normal head with strange bulging eyes.

The tall man continued with his explanation.

"I am Prince Cronus. We have taken DNA samples from your sisters and now it is your turn. Hades my master scientist and Seth my medical flyer will do that in a moment. Then we will continue with our mission to capture other people like you. Those with special abilities."

George had no idea what the alien meant by special abilities as he was more concerned with the robot which had silently floated up to the tube where he was imprisoned. In response George pressed himself against the back of the tube and felt panic rising in him like a beating drum pounding in his chest.

*

A short time later Prince Cronus, Hades and Seth, were in the control bridge of the flying saucer discussing the next stage of the mission. The room was filled with glowing screens, control consoles and flight seats. At the front there was a wide viewing window, which transformed from glass to metal whenever the pilot needed to see through it.

The prince stood in front of a glowing crystal sphere the size of a football, which hovered above one of the consoles. It was a globe of the Earth with tiny red dots which flickered on and off across the surface.

"The DNA tracker has located the next person we must abduct. After that there are nine more targets left to get."

Turning away from the sphere he gave orders to the auto pilot. This was a black pyramid shaped device the size of a rugby ball which was set into the top of the main console.

"Pilot, lock onto the nearest target and plot a direct course there."

The craft suddenly shot vertically into the sky above the school and silently disappeared into the clouds.

After a few moments the air close to where the craft had been hovering began to shimmer as if suffering a localised heatwave. Then abruptly another flying saucer appeared out of thin air. It was similar to Prince Cronus's craft except that its surface was silver and shiny rather than black and dull. After a moment it too shot rapidly into the sky in the exact direction the first one had flown and followed its route into the clouds.

Chapter Three

Anne was woken up by a loud bang and a violent shake. As soon as her eyes focused, she realised that she was still trapped in the tube. Looking around the room she saw that Cronus, Hades and Seth had gone, but immediately realised that there was something wrong with the craft she was imprisoned on. It was rising and falling abruptly, like an airplane when it passes through air turbulence. Once again it seemed to drop suddenly and she felt her stomach trying to force its way up through her mouth. Then the craft banked steeply to the right as if it was trying to fly away from something. In that moment of calm she looked around the room to see if any other glass tubes were occupied by prisoners. To her horror she saw that her brother and sister were trapped in tubes on the far wall.

Banging wildly on her tube she tried to make as much noise as she could, desperate to rouse them both. "Lucy, George! Wake up! Wake up!"

Once again the craft abruptly rose and then fell; however this time there was a distinct bang as if something had hit it. This impact woke Lucy and George. After a few seconds they regained their senses, saw Anne and began to bang on their glass tubes as well.

There was another loud bang and the craft lurched to the left again, this time into a steeper dive. Immediately all three children could feel the pull of the g-forces on their bodies, squashing them against the rear of their tubes.

The craft levelled out unexpectedly, and they were all thrown forward against the insides of their tubes. There was another sudden lurch and all the tubes sprang free from their ceiling clamps and toppled onto the floor. Stunned, the children span around like rag dolls as the tubes rolled around on the floor. However they also realised that the bottom of each tube had popped open. As soon as the tubes stopped rolling around, they scrambled out of the openings.

They all grabbed and hugged each other for a frantic moment, sobbing and crying. Finally Anne stepped back, calmed herself and took charge.

"We need to get out of this laboratory and find out where we are!"

"We've been sucked up into a big grey UFO," interrupted George loudly. "It beamed me up from outside the school."

Anne and Lucy looked shocked. With everything that had happened so far today, Anne had thought she could not be surprised with anything else. However being trapped on a UFO truly shocked even her!

She grabbed him and Lucy then ran out of the open door into a tubular metal corridor. The brightly lit route curved around the outer edge of the craft, and had a metal hand rail at waist height on its wall.

The trio ran along the corridor as fast as they could, their frantic footsteps echoing loudly, clanking like a hammer hitting a metal bar. Without warning the craft dropped suddenly and then rose steeply and banked hard to the left, forcing them to stagger from side to side.

"Hold on tightly to the hand rail!" ordered Anne, as she fought hard to keep her footing.

Grabbing it she pulled herself a few feet further forward, until she came across a small circular window in the outer hull of the craft.

Struggling to keep on their feet, the three of them held onto the rail and clustered around the window, eager to see where they were.

It was daylight and the craft they were trapped on was swooping in and out of banks of white cloud. Below them they could see a patchwork of green fields, roads and built up areas. Anne squinted to get a better view, trying to see if there were any landmarks which she could recognise.

"We're over London!" exclaimed Lucy first, spotting the Houses of Parliament.

Then another UFO came into view, swooping down at their craft and causing it to swerve.

"We're under attack. That's what is causing this craft to swerve all over the place!" shouted George triumphantly. "I knew it!"

Before the others could respond the craft dived again and then accelerated away, with the other UFO behind it. Anne put her head against the window and looked back at the craft chasing them. It was a classic flying saucer shape, over a hundred feet in diameter and shiny like polished silver.

For the next few minutes both craft swerved and sped amongst the clouds until they swooped low over another big city and rose high into the air again. "Now we're over Paris!" exclaimed George excitedly. "We must be flying incredibly fast!"

"What's that other UFO up to now?" said Lucy anxiously.

Even as the three of them watched, the shiny UFO drew closer and fired a bright beam of light at their craft.

They felt the judder of the impact run through the craft and it groaned as if in pain. In response the craft accelerated away again. Within moments they seemed to be zooming out across the sea.

"We need to find a way to get off this craft before it gets blown to pieces!" said Anne. "Let's see if we can find an escape pod or parachutes – anything!"

The craft accelerated again, pushing the three of them back against the metal wall and pinning them there with the g-force. After a few minutes the craft dropped steeply and slowed down. Able to move again the three children crowded around the window to see where they were now.

"The Pyramids!" exclaimed Anne. "We are in Egypt. And it only took a few minutes to get here from London!"

Suddenly the other craft dived into view and fired a blinding beam of energy at their craft. They were instantly thrown to the floor as the craft jolted from the impact of the weapon. This time there was also the sound of the hull tearing and then they were hit full in the face by the smell of burning metal. The hot, foul stink started to sting the back of their throats and caused their eyes to water. Anne held on to her brother and sister tightly, for she could guess what was going to happen next. They were going to crash. Crash into the desert.

The craft began to level off and slow down, as if it was attempting to make a soft landing. "Hold on! Just hold on!" she shouted over the roar of failing engines and air rushing past. She tensed her body, bracing for the violent impact. She held on tightly for what seemed an age, until for a second she thought that she had got it wrong. They were not going to crash?

Then the craft slammed into the desert, bouncing across its surface like a flat stone skimming across a pond. The three of them were thrown forwards and then backwards, dust and sand swirling around them. There was another loud metallic scream as a wide hole was torn in the outer side of the craft close to them. Immediately a blast of hot sand squirted in through the hole and lashed them.

Then the craft stopped abruptly, causing anything loose inside to be thrown forward. As soon as they had recovered from the ordeal, the three of them got up and hurled themselves out through the gaping hole in the side of the craft.

Anne landed face first in the sand and immediately pushed herself to her knees, eager to get as far away from the wreckage as possible. The sand stuck to her limbs and swimsuit like a layer of thin cement, which she brushed off with her hands as best she could. Lucy had landed bottom first and was already standing and knocking the sand from her skirt and boots. George had landed flat on his back and still lay stunned.

"We need to get away, NOW!" shouted Anne, as she sprinted over to him. Then she yanked him to his feet with both hands, just as Lucy came running over and joined them.

"The craft is on fire. The flames are spreading rapidly and it may explode at any moment!" shouted Lucy.

Anne looked in all directions for the best route to take. The craft was half buried in a small sand dune, with smoke billowing from the front of it. For miles in every other direction there was nothing but flat sand stretching as far as the eye could see. Then she looked up into the clear blue sky and noticed in the far distance a tiny glint of metal flying high in the east. Even squinting she could not see if it was the other UFO, or a rescue helicopter. Not waiting to find out, they held each other's hands and ran away from the crashed craft as fast as they could.

Chapter Four

Prince Cronus awoke in the wrecked control bridge of the crashed craft. The smell of burning metal and thick black smoke stung the back of his throat. He cursed loudly, sprang to his feet, and quickly brushed the burning sand off his suit as he surveyed the damage around him. The control bridge was smashed beyond repair. The medical robot Seth was lying lifeless at the far end of the room, torn into several jagged pieces. All of its electronic interior was exposed and spilling out onto the floor. Hades however was unharmed, apart from several cuts and tears in his suit. He coughed loudly to clear the dust from his throat and then stood up. Without saying anything, he immediately checked the instruments on the Control Matrix in front of him, his face a mixture of fear and anger. Finally he spoke.

"Our craft is beyond repair. The hull is breached in fifteen places and the main engine drive is off-line. The enemy craft got a direct hit on it. However some systems are still operating. Our scanners say the enemy craft is still in the area, circling for a final attack run. Even worse, all the DNA samples which we collected have also been destroyed in the attack." Hades then paused, hesitant about giving his master the final piece of bad news. "Even worse my prince, the three prisoners have somehow escaped and are running away from us across the desert."

Prince Cronus cursed out loud again and slammed his fists into the nearest control panel, denting it. "We must recapture them! We must have their DNA profiles or the whole mission is a failure."

Hades turned his attention to the Control Matrix. "The children may have a good head start on us, but we still have some undamaged equipment in the storage area which will help us catch them."

*

Anne, Lucy and George sprinted away from the crashed craft as fast as they could across the desert. As the athletic one, Anne could easily have left the other two behind, but she held back to grab their collars and keep pulling them forward. Every few minutes she would look back to see if the fire on the craft had spread.

This time she looked back and her heart sank as she saw something was happening. From around the far side of the half buried wreckage she saw a small, flat object emerging and flying towards them. An uncontrollable chill of fear tingled its way up her spine and for a moment she froze, causing the others to stop and look back as well. Anne squinted, trying to make out what the flying object was. However it was George who identified it first.

"It's Cronus and Hades standing on some sort of hover-board! They'll catch us in minutes at the speed they are moving!"

As Anne got a clearer view, she too saw that they were being chased by a shiny metal object. It looked like a large surf board with a hand rail running around its full length, with the prince and Hades standing at the front, leaning on the rail. Anne's heart suddenly jumped into her mouth and all three children screamed in unison at the sight of the object.

"Keep running! Keep running!" Anne shouted, as she yanked them both into motion again.

*

The hover-board gained more speed as it flew after them, scattering a trail of sand behind it.

"I need them alive. At least until I can get a good set of DNA samples," shouted the Prince loudly in order to be heard above the noise of the wind rushing past them.

In response Hades held up a large, unusual shaped hand gun. "That's not a problem, I'll use this immobiliser. It's not as good as the paralysing beam weapon we have on our crashed craft, but it will do."

Even as they spoke, the hover-board began to close in on the trio, gaining a bit of altitude in order to get the best attacking position.

Realising what they were going to do, the trio separated, each going in different directions. Anne continued to run directly ahead, to lead the hover-board after her, while Lucy and George escaped in opposite directions.

High above them, Hades gave a sly but confident grin. "Nice try children. But I can catch you all quite easily."

He calmly clipped a square cartridge into the rear of the gun and pointed it at George. The gun fired silently with no recoil and a spinning ball spat from the wide barrel. In a second the ball dramatically changed direction in midair and caught up with George. Behind him the ball suddenly opened into a wide sticky net and enveloped him, making a loud slap as the green strands wrapped around him and joined together. He immediately fell to the ground and lay stunned and motionless, like an insect wrapped in a spider's cocoon.

As the hover-board swooped low and levelled off just above the ground, Hades calmly loaded another cartridge into the weapon and aimed vaguely in Lucy's direction. There was no need to be a good shot, as the ball it fired would automatically home in on its target. A moment later the small ball opened up and caught her like a fly in the centre of a web, the impact knocking her off her feet. Caught in its twisting motion she span in the air and then fell forward and lay helpless on the ground as the sticky strands continued to tighten around her.

Anne stopped as soon as she realised what had happened and turned to run over to help George. But the way was blocked. Anne saw Hades standing at the front of the hover-board with his weapon pointed at her. Thinking that he needed to take direct aim at her, she turned and sprinted to the right to get out of the way. He fired and out of the corner of her eye she saw to her horror that the projectile had changed course in midair and was right behind her. Unlike her siblings, she stopped running and crouched down, hoping that the net would pass over her. But the rapidly opening net had a mind of its own and swerved lower to snare her. Trying to outsmart it she jumped up at the last moment, but it kept on target and swerved back up and slammed into her. She landed hard but managed to wriggle onto her knees and then stand upright, while still wrapped neck to toe in the sticky green strands. Determined not to give in, she refused to topple over and instead she called out words of support to George and Lucy. A moment later another net hit her full in the face and chest and knocked her onto her back. Hades was determined to capture her. Even as she lay stunned, she felt the weird sticky cords of the net closing around her like a straight jacket. In moments she found that she could not even sit up and look at her attacker. Even her efforts to shout to her brother and sister were cut short as some of the cords wrapped around her face like living things, until only her eyes could be seen. A moment later the hover-board arrived above her and came to a halt, silently poised like a bird of prey. Then the face of Hades looked down over the hand rail at her "Now we have them!"

Chapter Five

Anne's terror was replaced by confusion as a series of explosions threw billowing clouds of sand into the air all around them. As soon as her view cleared she saw that the hover-board was laying bent and upside down thirty feet away from her. Prince Cronus and Hades lay on their backs a distance away in the other direction, clearly stunned by the explosions.

Still trapped in the weird green net, she tried to roll over and get a better view of what was going on. Descending out of the clear blue sky she saw the rival UFO approaching. It hovered silently over them all, blotting out the sun for a moment and then landed, scattering a fine ring of sand as it touched down.

As she craned her neck to look at it, she saw that a hole had opened in its underside and two figures had floated out and landed on the ground. One was clearly humanoid while the other was round and mechanical.

The man was tall and thin, with chalk white skin and a narrow band of jet black hair, running from between his eyebrows over the top of his head to the back of his neck. Even at that distance Anne immediately realised that he looked similar to Cronus. He also had all-white eyes, with tiny pin-prick pupils.

Unlike the prince, he wore grey overalls lined with various pouches and pockets, with black boots and gloves. He also wore what looked like headphones, and what Anne guessed was some sort of mini back pack which allowed him to float.

The machine that was with him consisted of a metal sphere about six feet in diameter, with dozens of metallic tentacles extending from it. Some of the tentacles had sharp cutters on the ends while others had glowing tubes which Anne took to be guns.

The man floated across to Anne and touched down onto the sand next to her, while the spherical robot remained floating at head height as if to guard over them.

The man leaned down over her "We are here to save you, your sister and brother. We are also here to stop and arrest Prince Cronus and Master Scientist Hades."

As if acting on a mental command the robot floated across the undulating sand then stopped and hovered close to the prince and Hades. Meanwhile the man stood over Anne and pointed a black tube at her. To her it looked like a torch without a glass bulb at the end. Out of it suddenly sprayed a cloud of green smoke which closed around her like a large blanket. Almost straight away she felt the net around her body starting to loosen. Determined to get free, she pushed against it and felt the strands melting and falling off. As quickly as she could she tore the rest of the net off and stood up. Meanwhile the man had already floated away from her and had sprayed Lucy and George with the green smoke. Seeing how she had escaped, they too were starting to tear themselves free.

"Who are you?" demanded Anne to the man as he turned and floated back towards her.

"Time for a detailed explanation later. First we must get Prince Cronus and Hades locked up on our craft. Once we have done that then we can get you three home to safety and give you a full explanation of what is happening and why they kidnapped you".

Anne took a step back from him, noting how similar he looked to the prince. They were clearly of the same race. "There is no way we are getting into your flying saucer. How do we know you're not some rival group of aliens trying to snatch us for your own weird experiments?"

The man nodded as if he understood her concerns, but he seemed nervous and kept looking away from her to study the sky. Was he unable to make eye contact because he was avoiding her questions, or was he scared of something? She was not sure.

Frustrated by her indecision, he suddenly moved closer to her and a stern look formed on his face. "I could easily force you onto my craft, but I would prefer that you come with us willingly. It is for your own safety."

Without warning the ground around them exploded; throwing great columns of sand into the air. Anne instinctively stood closer to the man for protection, when she realised that he was equally surprised by the explosions. They both covered their mouths and noses with their hands to keep out the worst of the swirling sand. Coughing and spluttering they stood still and looked in the direction of the explosions and strained to see through the smoke.

Then as the swirling sand and smoke cleared they saw two shapes approaching them. Anne immediately stepped forward anxiously hoping it was Lucy and George.

Abruptly the man next to Anne put his arm out in front of her and stopped her. "Keep back girl; it's the enemy!"

Before she could respond, the last of the smoke blew away to reveal who was approaching.

It was a woman and yet another floating robot!

The woman had an Egyptian look about her, with straight black hair and distinctive eye make-up. However her face and features were also similar to Prince Cronus. She was clearly of the same race as the prince. She wore a skin tight silver metallic outfit with red belt, boots and gloves. Various small pieces of electronic equipment were fitted to the outfit. She was tall, athletic and carried herself like someone full of confidence and used to getting what she wanted.

The robot was a floating metal box about a foot square. Out of it extended six thin metal pipes, one from each side. Each pipe was a foot long. Anne thought that it looked silly in comparison to the multi-tentacle robot that the man standing next to her had brought with him.

As the last of the swirling sand blew away she saw that another UFO had appeared in the sky. It was identical to the crashed one and hovered menacingly several hundred feet away from them.

The man standing next to Anne immediately pressed a sensor on his wrist control and a transparent blue energy field formed around him, Anne and his landed craft.

"Now they cannot harm us or my spacecraft," he stated confidently. "My name is Dagr and I am here to help you Anne." Pointing at the approaching woman he continued to talk to Anne. "She is Princess Sekmet and that is one of her combat drones. She is sister to Prince Cronus. This was why I wanted you all to come with me straight away. We knew that the enemy had another craft and would come to rescue Cronus and re-capture you!"

Anne recognised Sekmet as the name of the ancient Egyptian goddess of war and terror. She also remembered that Dagr was a Nordic god of light. All of the aliens seemed to have names based on ancient human legends. Looking at the princess, Anne could easily believe that the striking looking woman was a person to be reckoned with. Meanwhile the man next to Anne seemed to be genuinely concerned about her and her siblings.

Princess Sekmet had anticipated that Dagr would activate his energy field, so instead she pointed her right arm at Prince Cronus and Hades. Immediately her square combat drone obeyed her mental command and flew over to Dagr's spherical robot, which was still guarding over the prince and Hades. The combat drone immediately fired several bolts of energy at the spherical robot from one of its pipes. However Dagr's robot had already raised a protective energy shield between them, causing the bolts to bounce off harmlessly.

Meanwhile the princess turned towards Dagr who still stood next to Anne. "I don't know how you discovered we had woken from our long hibernation, but you cannot stop us. I have come to rescue my brother and Hades and then take the three humans with us. You will not save them."

On her mental command, the combat drone immediately flew high into the sky and circled Dagr's robot. Then it started to fire at the robot while being careful to avoid hitting Prince Cronus or Hades by mistake.

Anne almost sniggered as she watched the strange square drone attacking the much larger spherical robot. "Surely that small thing can't win against your multi-armed robot, Dagr?"

The man shook his head in response. "Do not be fooled by the difference in size and looks. The princess's combat drone is just one of a network of deadly weapons which she has."

Even as he said this, the drone swooped and changed position, avoiding a hail of projectiles which spat from some of Dagr's robot's twisting tentacles. In response the drone fired a narrow sonic blast from one of its pipes. The blast passed straight through the protective energy shield and hit the robot hard. The sphere tumbled backwards, momentarily out of control, its energy shield short circuiting and vanishing.

As the two robots were engrossed in their battle, Prince Cronus and Hades seized the opportunity to escape and ran towards the princess, their faces a mixture of relief and anger. As soon as they got next to her, she gave them a scornful look, angry that they had crashed their ship. They stood in silence behind her, realising that she was furious with them. Without saying a word she pressed a control on the back of her left hand and the two of them vanished in a flash of green light; teleported up into her hovering craft.

Dagr stepped forward to shield Anne. "The princess is using her drone to distract mine and she's succeeded in teleporting those two safely up into her ship. I know her tactics: next she's going to try and recapture you three children!"

Even as he spoke, the woman floated in the direction of Lucy and George, intending to block their escape route to Anne and Dagr.

"We've got to save them!" shouted Anne at the top of her voice as she attempted to dash past Dagr.

In response to her shout, Sekmet stopped her approach to Lucy and George and turned to block Anne by firing a series of laser blasts from a weapon around her right wrist. The weapon looked like a thick silver bracelet with multicoloured jewels set in it. Even though the lasers bounced harmlessly off Dagr's force field, Anne could not help wincing and turning her head away.

"While we are inside my craft's protective energy shield Sekmet cannot harm us," said Dagr. "But unfortunately we are unable to help Lucy and George."

"You have to do something. You can't let her get them!" screamed Anne in desperation.

"Don't worry I won't let her get them," replied Dagr. "I'll command my robot to intercept the princess!"

Immediately responding to the mental command, Dagr's robot smashed into the princess's combat drone and knocked it out of the way. The drone was momentarily disabled as it slammed into the sand, allowing precious time for Dagr's robot to fly across the sand towards the princess.

Sekmet immediately stopped and turned and fired at it with her wrist weapons, but the first shots bounced off its energy shield. As it got closer it changed course and circled around her, swiping and slashing at her with its razor sharp pincers and cutters. Undeterred, she stood calmly and fired her sonic weapon at it, knocking Dagr's robot backwards. Meanwhile her combat drone had freed itself from the sand and was speeding towards its mistress. The moment it arrived they both fired a combined cross fire blast at Dagr's robot. The explosions brought it to a stop, then it shuddered, spluttered and dropped to the ground and cracked open. Seconds later thick black smoke began to billow from its cracked casing.

Seizing the moment, Lucy and George ran towards Anne, trying to escape while the princess and her drone were distracted by the burning robot.

Just as they thought they had escaped, the princess pointed her left hand at George and her green wrist band fired a thin cable at him. The end of the cable wrapped around his right ankle and she yanked him backwards to fall face first onto the ground. Next she pressed a control on the back of her hand and the cable retracted, dragging him backwards to her. In seconds he was within reach, so she detached the cable and grabbed him around the waist and pulled him to his feet. Kicking and shouting he struggled to get free, but she strengthened her grip with one arm, and pressed her teleport control with the other. Next there was a green flash and she, George and her combat drone vanished.

"She's got George!" exclaimed Anne just as Lucy reached her and fell exhausted to the ground next to Dagr. Even before Dagr could act to save George, the rival flying saucer rose high into the bright blue sky and sped east. Still just in sight, it stopped and hovered over the wreckage of the crashed flying saucer. Suddenly it fired down a wide beam of red light and what was left of the wreckage was vaporised into a cloud of steam. Having destroyed all evidence of the wreckage, Sekmet's flying saucer sped out of sight at incredible speed.

Chapter Six

Before they could catch their breath, Anne and her sister vanished from the desert in a burst of light and were teleported on board the landed flying saucer along with Dagr and his damaged robot.

They reappeared in a small circular room somewhere inside the craft. Anne, Lucy and Dagr stood motionless for a moment as the weird sensation of their bodies being atomised and re-formed wore off. The robot however collapsed loudly onto the metal floor in a smoking heap. Finally it made a short high pitched whistle, like steam escaping from a kettle, and then fell apart like the segments of an orange, beyond repair.

As soon as she had fully materialised, Anne took a deep breath and then launched into a barrage of questions "Who are you really? Where is George? Tell us what is going on!"

"Yes! Who are you and what's happened to our brother?"added Lucy equally loudly, after taking a few deep breaths to calm herself.

Meanwhile Anne turned and stood directly in front of Dagr, looking him sternly in the eye. "Tell us!"

Dagr stroked his chin with his right hand and considered what he should say. "I promise I will explain a great many things and then everything will become clear to you. But before we go any further you two need to change into proper high pressure flying suits. You have to do this because we are going to chase after the other spacecraft at speeds your unprotected bodies will not be able to withstand."

Before either of them could move, two beams of light shone down from the ceiling and engulfed both girls. Next they felt themselves held in place by invisible energy and finally a glowing ring of light began to descend over them. Anne fought against the urge to panic as she realised that Dagr was different to Prince Cronus. As the glow moved down it atomised their clothes and instantly replaced them with skin tight flight suits. Anne thought that they were like divers' wet suits, with pockets, boots and belt all built in. Hers was a pale red while Lucy's was pale yellow.

Having her swim suit atomised was a welcome relief to Anne as it had become torn and sand had become trapped in awkward places. Lucy was also secretly glad to be rid of her school clothes, as she had dressed for a colder climate than the Sahara, and hated the way the sand had crept into every fold of the material. With a finishing flicker the two beams of light vanished, leaving the girls in their new purpose made flight suits.

Dagr looked at them approvingly, satisfied that they were now properly protected. "Now come with me and I will explain what is happening and how we are going to rescue your brother George."

Dagr took them into a much larger room. It was circular and had walls like mirrors. In the ceiling there was a series of lenses like mini projectors. He snapped his fingers and a series of holographic images beamed down from the ceiling and surrounded them all.

"My name is Commander Dagr and I am in charge of this spacecraft and the mission to stop the prince and princess."

At that moment a door opened in the far wall and a tall, thin woman strode in. She was dressed in a similar flight suit to Dagr, but her facial features were less harsh than his. Anne thought that she looked elf-like, as well as being strong and elegant. "I am Bridgid, deputy commander of this craft and mission."

From her studies, Lucy vaguely remembered that Bridgid was an ancient Celtic solar goddess; and wondered how all these weird looking aliens had names based on mythical human gods.

Commander Dagr stood at the centre of the room and began. "The three of you children were targeted deliberately. You are part of a selected number of people all over the world who will be kidnapped by the prince and princess today."

Anne stepped protectively in front of her sister "Why? Why would we be targeted by alien kidnappers?"

Dagr made a gesture with his hands and images of the prince and princess appeared, followed by a montage of people who looked like them.

"Firstly Prince Cronus and Princess Sekmet are not aliens. Secondly neither I nor Bridgid are aliens. We all originally come from Earth."

Even before the girls could react to the astonishing revelation; he pointed directly at Anne and her sister.

"You and your brother are long lost descendents of ancient Atlantis. Ten thousand years ago the highly advanced Island-civilisation of Atlantis suddenly exploded and sank without trace. The few survivors were thrown into confusion and had to take emergency action. Most of the survivors, just a few hundred, were able to escape in a small fleet of spacecraft like this one. They left the Earth forever because it had been thrown back into chaos. Instead they travelled across the galaxy to establish a new home on a distant planet. I am one of the descendents of those survivors and that distant planet is where I have come from. Its name and location is a secret. All of us on this craft are descendents of those original survivors from Atlantis and we have now returned to Earth to help you."

For the first time Lucy began to engage in the conversation, putting her questioning mind to work on all the information that was being thrown at them.

"Why are you helping us, if the prince and princess are the same as you?"

The commander made another gesture and more moving holographic images appeared around them.

"When Atlantis sank a very small group of survivors did not come with us into space. Instead they escaped to great caverns and tunnels which had been built deep in the Earth. The tunnels were filled with experimental laboratories and research facilities. This is what became known as the Hollow Earth. These survivors were led by the children of High King Zektor, who was the leader of Atlantis when it exploded. The children were Prince Cronus and Princess Sekmet. In order to survive the destruction on the surface they put themselves into suspended animation. Now they have woken up! The prince was the one who captured you and the princess is the one who just rescued him and snatched George."

*

Inside Sekmet's spacecraft, she, the prince and Hades were studying George. He was lying unconscious on an examination table inside a transparent tube. The tube was lying flat on a metal frame with wires and pipes coming out of the top and bottom which were connected to stacks of flashing instruments on the floor under the frame.

Hades was standing by controls which were on a nearby wall panel. "This boy is remarkable! The ancient Atlantis DNA is exceptionally strong in him!"

The princess took a close look for herself at the results of the new tests "What are you saying Hades?"

The little man pointed at the flat screen set into the wall close to him. "We do not need to kidnap any more people. The Atlantis gene George has is so strong that now we only need him to revive all our Giants and Titans!"

Princess Sekmet thought for a moment. "So all we now need to carry out our plans is a fully charged power module. The historical records in our database show where they were all hidden ten thousand years ago. And our onboard sensors have detected where the only remaining fully energised one is located."

Turning to her brother she gave him a confident smile. "Set course for the Bermuda Triangle!"

Chapter Seven

Back on Dagr's craft, he paced around the room, trying to explain more about the destruction of Atlantis and the fate of its survivors.

"We only have fragments of information but our historical records show that Dinvad, the scientist supreme of Atlantis, and Jaxar, its top agent, took the zodiac crystals which powered Atlantis and hid them across time in order to stop the Earth being destroyed by dimension shocks. Although the twelve zodiac crystals were very powerful, their use was attracting destructive dimension shocks to Atlantis. By hiding them across time they saved the Earth; but not in time to prevent Atlantis being destroyed by the minor dimension shocks remaining in the area. We have no idea where the crystals went, but local prophecies suggested that a human boy would eventually re-discover them far in the future!"

Anne started to pace around among the moving images. "Ok. Even if Lucy and I believe you, how do we fit into all this?"

In response the deputy commander gestured with her hands and another series of images began to float around them all. "You fit in like this. There was a third group of survivors to escape the destruction of Atlantis. Just before it exploded and sank, a small number escaped and scattered across the Earth's surface and managed to reach areas where there were a few civilised humans; such as Egypt, British Isles, and China. Had Atlantis not exploded then these outposts would have become the first in a network of colonies established across the planet. However this third group of survivors merged with the local humans and it is their DNA heritage that secretly continues undetected in a few human families today. Your family has a trace of that DNA. You are descendents of Atlantis!"

Anne and Lucy stood in complete shock, as images of weird alien landscapes and strange people in even stranger costumes swirled around them.

Anne walked up to Bridgid, filled with a mixture of confusion and fear. "But why are they trying to kidnap us? After all these thousands of years?"

The deputy continued. "Recent events on Earth have shocked the prince, princess and their handful of scientists out of suspended animation. Events which have sent them after you and other families like yours."

"What events?" said Lucy frowning.

Bridgid continued. "Recently there have been simultaneous volcanic eruptions all over the world: Iceland, Antarctica, Hawaii, Japan, Russia, Sicily. You must have seen something about it on your Earth news. These eruptions seem to have triggered seismic activity in the Hollow Earth and activated all the equipment down there, including the suspended animation devices. The prince, princess and their scientists are Atlantis purebloods. Now they have been awakened they are hunting after the few others on the planet's surface who have their DNA. People like you."

At that point the deputy commander turned to exit through the open door she had come in by.

"I must check the navigation and communications sensors. We still need to try and locate where Sekmet's craft is."

Lucy turned and continued the anxious conversation with Dagr. "The prince and princess may need more DNA but that still doesn't explain why they need us," she insisted.

Then Dagr pointed at the new images which were floating around them all. "They will use the DNA from you and the other families on the surface to bring the Titans and Giants back to life. They will use the immense power of those monsters to take over the world. It will also make the prince, princess and their supporters immune from modern day surface world diseases."

Academic Lucy shook her head and looked around at the monstrous images which had begun to be projected around them. She knew her history well and recognised some. "Titans and Giants? Are you referring to Greek myths?" she said to him.

He nodded and pointed at some of the images. "Yes. Greek mythology is based on the legends of Atlantis. How it was created, its first leaders, the twelve crystal Lords and the experiments which took place in the Hollow Earth tunnels. Greek mythology states that Gaea and Uranus lived on Mount Olympus, the home of the gods on Earth. Soon they became parents to twelve gigantic children, who were so powerful that their father Uranus feared them. These Giants were called Titans. To stop them using their power against him, Uranus hurled them into a dark abyss called Tartarus and imprisoned them there. The dark chasm was situated deep under the earth. This is where the legends of Hades and Tartarus come from. Uranus's sons were called Oceanus, Coeus, Creus, Hyperion, Lapetus, and Cronus. The daughters were called Ilia, Rhea, Themis, Thetis, Muemosyne and Phoebe.

Cronus managed to escape from Tartarus and overcame his father and freed his brothers and sisters from their underworld prison.

However Cronus had been cursed by his father Uranus, warning that he too would be overthrown by his own children! So each time his wife Rhea had a child he swallowed the child whole. But finally when her youngest son Zeus was born she tricked Cronus and sent Zeus to safety in secret. Eventually Zeus returned and defeated his father in a great battle. Zeus then forced Cronus to vomit up the other children. Zeus then gave his brothers and sisters a share of his earthly domain. Some of the titan brothers and sisters of Cronus also gave their allegiance to Zeus. But others would not do so and so began another terrible war, called the Revolt of the Titans. The war lasted ten years and the only way Zeus could win was to release from the underworld the Cyclops and Hecatoncheires. The Cyclops had thunderbolts and Hecatoncheires had a hundred-handed army. Eventually Zeus won and the Titans were thrown back into Tartarus.

Zeus had hardly overcome the Titans when he found himself in a new war against the Giants. These were monstrous mutants created in the underworld. They had legs like serpents, feet like the heads of snakes. After another long war involving massive destruction, the Giants were defeated.

But the crisis did not end there. Gaea raised a final monster called Typhoeus against Zeus. The monster had been manufactured in Tartarus. After capture, Zeus finally overcame the monster and a long period of peace followed. That was all myth but based on real ancient events.

Greek, Roman even Celtic and Egyptian legends and myths are based on human folk memories of Atlantis. But the facts are that, Atlantis may have been destroyed ten thousand years ago, but Tartarus is a very real place which still exists today deep in the earth. Rumours and myths call it the Hollow Earth. And that is where Prince Cronus and Princess Sekmet have their secret base."

Lucy considered what he had said for a moment and then continued, "If what you are saying is true, how did your people find out about Sekmet waking from suspended animation; if you are on a planet light years away from Earth?"

Dagr nodded and responded to her question. "On my planet we detected the simultaneous eruptions. We have some high powered warning beacons hidden on Earth, designed to alert us if humans reach a certain technological level; or if there is any other strange activity. Our beacons alerted our home world to the eruptions and then that the ancient machinery underground had re-activated. We immediately launched this spacecraft to come here to stop them."

"And have you? Have you stopped them by rescuing me and Lucy?" said Anne, with a look of desperation in her eyes.

Dagr shook his head "We have only delayed them but not stopped them. Even though they have George, they will still have to go after the other humans who have inherited the Atlantis DNA. On their craft, they have a DNA tracker to locate and hunt for the people, just like they tracked you down. As well as that they will then have to get a fully charged power module. Our sensors showed that the one in the Hollow Earth has been depleted by keeping the suspended animation equipment running for ten thousand years. Back in those ancient times several other power modules were hidden across the Earth, but our warning beacons tell us that there is only one which is still active and it is hidden in the Bermuda Triangle".

"I just want to know how do we stop them and rescue George?" interrupted Anne, losing patience with the complicated history lesson Dagr was giving them.

The man sensed the two girls' frustration and speeded up his explanation. "The way to thwart the prince and princess's plans is to either stop them kidnapping anymore people or for us to get the power module from the Bermuda Triangle first!" he responded.

Suddenly Bridgid came back into the room. She had an anxious look on her face and was determined to interrupt them. "We have just intercepted a secret communication between the princess's craft and her Hollow Earth base. It states that they have George on board and have re–tested him for the special DNA. The test indicates that his DNA has such strong Atlantis markers that they do not need to take any more prisoners. He is powerful enough to do everything for them. Now they only need to get the power module from the Bermuda Triangle. Once they have it they intend to return directly to the Hollow Earth and use it and George to re-animate the Titans and Giants!"

Commander Dagr shook his head in sorrow. "This is disastrous news! We must stop them at all costs. Bridgid, abandon your scans to find the enemy craft and set course directly for the Bermuda Triangle. We must get the power module before the enemy gets it!"

Anne interrupted him "Why do you have to do this alone? Why can't you tell the United Nations or someone with military power like NATO? They could blow up one lone UFO or bombard the entrances to the Hollow Earth".

Dagr shook his head again. "No. For a number of reasons. Firstly humans must never discover that we exist or where our home planet is. They would treat us as a threat and attack us as well. Secondly human governments would steal our advanced technology and squabble amongst themselves. They would use our technology in wars against each other. Thirdly, even if they did not conspire to do that, your brother would certainly be killed if the humans launched a mass attack on the Hollow Earth!"

Anne and Lucy nodded in agreement, realising that telling other people could lead to George's doom.

"There is also the added danger that if you reveal to your government the secret of ancient Atlantis or that you have special DNA, then various secret government agencies around the world would kidnap you both for themselves. You and the others like you would be experimented on, in order to learn if you have special powers or immunities from illnesses. Because you have Atlantis genes there is a danger that they would never let you go. You would become guinea pigs for secret experiments. No! You have to keep this mission a secret. Even your friends and family must never know!"

"If we want to save George and stop the prince and princess, we have to do this by ourselves and in secret. What is more we have less than twelve hours to stop them or it will be too late!"

Raising his voice Dagr gave an urgent order "Navigator robot – set course for the Bermuda Triangle!"

Deputy Commander Bridgid turned and headed for the control bridge "I have already set course for the triangle at full speed. We should be there in ten Earth minutes."

Chapter Eight

George woke up with a jolt, instantly aware that he was no longer standing in the desert. He was also aware that he had a throbbing headache and felt bruised all over. He sat up and found that he was wearing a red boiler suit with red boots and metal belt. Looking around he saw that he was sat on a metal bed which was attached to the wall of what he guessed was a cell. The roof, floor and walls of the cell were all made of dull metal, except one wall which had floor to ceiling glass. He also noted that there was no door, but could feel a slight vibration in the floor and could smell what he thought was hot metal.

Sitting up on the bed he began to think about what had happened. One minute he had been prisoner in a hostile flying saucer, then it had crashed and he had escaped across the desert. The next minute he woke up in this cell. Considering he had been kidnapped by what he assumed were aliens, he felt surprisingly calm. He guessed that they had drugged him in some way so that he would not panic. Then his thoughts turned to his sisters. Had they been captured as well? Were they on this flying saucer in cells of their own? Then he changed the track of his thoughts again. Was he even on the second hostile flying saucer? Was he even on Earth?

At the back of his mind he knew that he should be worried about all these things, even be on the verge of panic. But he wasn't. He was calm and relaxed.

*

From outside the cell Hades, Cronus and Sekmet observed George through the secret one way window set in the far wall.

Hades voiced his thoughts first. "I think that the boy has much more potential which we can exploit. He already has significant computer skills, which I could enhance. I could also enhance his DNA profile and make it more powerful, so he can use it to re-animate a lot more of our Titans and Giants."

Sekmet interrupted "Very well, proceed with the enhancements. But I also want you to hypnotise the boy. He will work better for us if he is willing. If we can get him on our side, his enhanced abilities will give us great power!"

*

Anne marvelled at the technology that surrounded her. She was sat in a floating airplane-type seat in the main control bridge of the Dagr's spacecraft, surrounded by various floating control boards. Some boards were magnetically tethered to the same spot, while others were free to drift slowly around the bridge in an organised pattern, only stopping when one of the crew needed to make an adjustment. The crew consisted of one other male who looked like Dagr and a robot navigator. The robot consisted of five transparent spheres, each the size of a football, joined together in a line, like a snake. Each sphere-segment glowed with a different colour and had numerous wires protruding, which all moved independently, like the tentacles on a sea-anemone. It hovered among the moving controls, observing data and silently giving instructions. The man was also connected into the craft's controls by wires which extended from his head and neck. Anne had no idea what they were doing or how any of it worked, but as long as they arrived at the Bermuda Triangle before the prince and princess she did not care.

Lucy however was keen to ask as many questions as possible and understand as much as she could. She wanted to absorb the most she could of this futuristic-yet-age-old technology as possible. She was also keen to understand as much as possible of her mystery heritage from ancient Atlantis. Anne however was focused on the mission. The mission to rescue her brother and stop the Hollow Earth Atlantis survivors from gaining the power to revive the Titans and Giants.

Next an electronic voice interrupted them all. "We have arrived over the point of the Atlantic Ocean where the centre of the Bermuda Triangle is."

Lucy knew about the Bermuda Triangle only by reputation. According to UFO fanatics it was a mysterious area of the Atlantic Ocean where for hundreds of years boats and aircraft had vanished without trace. Some strange power was rumoured to be deep on the ocean floor, sucking things down.

Below the craft the bright blue sea sparkled in the early morning sunshine. It was relatively calm with small waves and no ships in sight.

"How are we going to get underwater, let alone to the sea bed?" said Anne.

The commander smiled at the girl's naivety. "This craft was designed to survive the extremes of faster than light travel over great distances, the crushing depths of the ocean cannot harm us."

He snapped his fingers and one of the floating control panels stopped in front of him. Next he blinked at it in a set pattern and the various lights on it changed colour.

Straight away the craft dropped vertically into the ocean and began to sink rapidly out of sight. In seconds it was steering a steep course down to the hidden power module.

Still keen to learn as much as possible, Lucy looked out through one of the windows in the side of the control bridge "It's pitch black down here, how are we supposed to see anything?"

As if in answer, the outer hull of the craft burst into brilliant light, exposing everything for hundreds of yards around it. As the craft continued to descend, a fantastic structure began to come into view. A structure the size of a small city made out of white crystal emerged in front of them. It consisted of twelve long fingers of crystal each the size of sky scrapers, all fanning out in different directions from a single base set into the sea bed.

Commander Dagr pointed at it from the control bridge. "It was grown by the scientists of ancient Atlantis. It is called Nun. After Atlantis exploded and humans took over the Earth, Nun became the name of an ancient Egyptian God. Nun came to mean water, the primeval water of chaos from which emerged creation. Egyptian legend was correct; this was a genetic engineering research facility. Several such crystal sites were grown in secret locations all over the world, but this is the only one which survived the great disaster which destroyed Atlantis. It was a research and development facility, working to harness the power of the crystals."

Bridgid stepped forward. "Our instruments have detected an active power source inside the structure. This is what causes the mysterious disappearances of aeroplanes and ships which take place on the surface.

This is what has given rise to the legend of the Bermuda Triangle."

Lucy frowned with concern. "How do we get inside? Swim or by mini-sub?"

Again Dagr chuckled. "No, our teleportation device can transfer us through water as easily as air. Prepare to be transported across to the building the moment we come to a stop."

*

Anne and Dagr appeared inside the underwater structure in a flash of green light. She immediately saw that the inside of the building was like the outside, a vast complex of crystals of different colours set at different angles. She and the commander had materialised into an area where several corridors intersected and formed a meeting point.

Anne gaped open mouthed at the size of the structure and how the crystals merged into each other like strange interlocking mirrors. Even more shocking, she realised that the smooth floor they were standing on was transparent and she could see a vast chamber below. To her, what looked like vast roots made out of multi-coloured crystal had burrowed down into the dark sea bed, holding Nun in place.

Dagr continued, "The structure was grown by our ancient ancestors. They discovered how to use the natural crystalline structure of the Earth and encourage crystals to grow and change. They discovered and harnessed many natural energies of the Earth."

Dagr stopped and checked that both of their communication devices worked. Firstly to talk to each other if separated and secondly back to the craft floating outside the structure if needed. They both had micro ear pieces and back-up wrist devices.

"Where is the power module?" said Anne, suddenly feeling vulnerable inside this vast alien structure.

"That way," he responded calmly, pointing towards a metal door. As they approached, the door slid open and they were swept off their feet and sucked through. Before they realised what was happening they flew vertically up a glass tube and were then swept sideways into a small domed room. The door to the tube closed behind them silently and Anne saw that the walls of the room were made of millions of tiny gems. However she was alarmed to see that there was no exit. Dagr looked at her and gave a reassuring smile. "Do not concern yourself; these are typical parts of the security system."

Even as he spoke the part of the wall nearest to them melted away to reveal a square corridor. Without hesitation Dagr strode into it, followed closely by an apprehensive Anne.

The corridor led to a large square room with mirrored walls, ceiling and floor. "What now?" murmured Anne. As if in response to her question, a holographic figure appeared in front of them.

It was the figure of a man. He was a tall grand old man with long, braided white beard and moustache. His hair however was cut short and angular. He was dressed in a knee-length white robe, trimmed with strange blue and gold symbols and wore sturdy, knee length boots.

"Greetings, I am a holographic image of Dinvad the scientist supreme of Atlantis. I have stationed this image of myself here as part of the Nun complex defence system. Only someone of pure Atlantis blood is permitted to go beyond and get the power module."

Anne stood next to the commander, not knowing what would happen next. Trying to make sense of things, Dagr whispered discreetly to her, "Dinvad was the chief scientist in Atlantis ten thousand years ago, at the time when it exploded and sank. He must have created holographs of himself to guard all the secret scientific outposts he had created."

Without making a sound, the holograph walked towards them and stopped in front of Dagr. Suddenly a beam of white light shone from the ceiling and scanned Dagr up and down several times.

"Negative!" You are not of pure Atlantis blood!" stated the holographic image sternly.

Before either of them could respond to the shock refusal, the beam scanned Anne. She held her breath, not knowing how to react.

"Access granted. Atlantis pure blood detected."

The holograph stepped back from them. "The girl can proceed to the inner sanctum, while the man must remain out here."

The holographic image of Dinvad gestured towards the far wall and it began to shimmer.

Dagr hesitated for a moment. "I am worried that you will be alone. You have no understanding of this ancient technology. Nor do I understand why you were chosen instead of me."

Anne anxiously stepped forward and made her way past the hologram to the shimmering wall. "For some weird reason the security system has identified me as the only person who can get the power module, so the sooner I go in and get it the better, before the prince and princess arrive."

As she approached the wall, she extended her right arm and pushed. To her surprise there was no resistance and she walked through the wall as if was not there. Behind her the wall immediately turned solid and the hologram of Dinvad vanished. There was no going back.

Chapter Nine

On board Sekmet's craft, Hades was supervising the enhancement procedures he was performing on George. They were in a room which looked like a hospital operating theatre. At one end there was a tall transparent tube filled with clear green liquid. In the liquid floated an unconscious George, wearing a breathing mask connected to tubes.

Hades was dressed in a full white medical gown and mask. He sat in a black swivelling chair surrounded by floating control panels, speaking out loud to his personal computer which was set into the ceiling.

"Electrical stimulation of the subject George Cristal begins now. My aim is to enhance his abilities so he can interface with Atlantis technology."

The tube began to fill with millions of tiny bubbles and the boy began to sway in the flow of the liquid like a slow motion rag doll. Gradually his body began to glow as the alien technology started to penetrate it.

Hades studied his instruments intently, anxious to ensure that the boy got the maximum exposure, while remaining safe. He did not want the boy perishing before he could re-animate the Giants and Titans for his prince and princess!

*

Inside the sanctum Anne found that things were not as she was expecting. Not that she had any idea what to expect! Everything was upside down. She had stepped out onto what she guessed was the ceiling of a square room. In the middle there was a crystal pillar about chest high and set on top of it was a glass cube about a foot square. Suspended perfectly at the centre of the cube was the power module. The device was a golden square six inches across. Each of the four points of the square had an egg sized crystal. The four crystals represented the four elements of Air, Water, Earth and Fire. The golden square was engraved with strange numbers and what looked like micro-circuitry. The module pulsated with the energy of the four crystals, alternating between white, blue, green and red. Anne was immediately captivated by it.

Suddenly her ear communicator crackled into life.

"Are you alright Anne? Are you inside yet?" said the commander anxiously.

"I'm OK, but the room seems to be upside down. I'm standing on a flat surface which looks like it's the ceiling. The power module is locked inside a glass box on a pillar growing out of the floor – which is above me."

Dagr's voice crackled back. "Anti-gravity security rooms were a speciality of ancient Atlantis technology. Even the twelve zodiac crystals which protected and powered Atlantis were contained in these types of security rooms. But without anti-gravity equipment you will not be able to float up to get the power module."

"And you didn't think that it might be a good idea to bring such equipment with us," she retorted sarcastically, "knowing that this was a likely security measure which we would encounter?"

Before Dagr could respond, the hologram of Dinvad appeared next to Anne. "In order to succeed you must pass two tests. First a mental test, then a physical test. And you only have five minutes to pass them."

"And if I fail?" gasped Anne, realising that she was trapped inside and had no other choice.

"The multi-directional lasers hidden in the ceiling will cut you into very tiny pieces," responded the hologram coldly.

Hearing the conversation on his headset the commander crackled a warning over the communicator. "Beware Anne; I cannot get in there to help you."

The hologram smiled at her and pointed to a midair position in front of her where a mathematical equation in glowing figures and lines had just appeared.

Anne's jaw dropped in despair. "Maths? I hate maths! Especially as I am useless at it!"

Dagr's voice crackled over the communications device again. "Don't panic. This is a test of you on a higher level, not just to solve some mathematical equation. It was especially designed for someone with pure Atlantis blood. Somewhere in you there must be the ability to solve this; otherwise you would not have been allowed access to the inner sanctum!"

Suddenly Lucy's voice came over the radio. "Anne our genetic abilities have obviously been split over the millennia. You have the brawn and I have the brains."

Anne sneered at her sister's statement of the obvious. "Ok I'll scan the image so you can see it."

The wrist communicator she wore also had the ability to scan and transmit things that it saw, so Anne pointed it at the floating equation.

"Well? Can you decode it Lucy?" said Anne knowing that she only had a few minutes left to live. Meanwhile the hologram stood close by and grinned at her knowingly.

In the craft floating outside, Lucy frantically studied the 3D image. "It's a complex code, not unlike a mega crossword. The sort of thing I enjoy doing every day. Tell your holographic friend the answer is x over y to the power of 3."

Before Anne could even try to understand the answer, the image of Dinvad nodded and smiled. "Answer accepted. First test complete!"

Anne took a pace towards him. "What's next? What's the physical test?"

Dinvad grinned. "Do you have the physical grit and determination to reach the power module. You have two minutes left. I will leave you now. If you succeed you do not need me. If you fail, you will be very dead and not care anymore! Good bye and good luck!"

The moment he vanished the room was suddenly filled with water. Not pouring in through holes or vents but suddenly appearing as if it had all been teleported into the room in one mass. Straight away Anne was swept off her feet and caught in the vortex of swirling liquid. Luckily the moment the water had appeared she had instinctively taken a deep breath of the disappearing air and begun to swim towards the glass cube. Despite the power of the swirling water it still sat fixed to the crystal pillar. Realising that she had little breath left in her and seconds before the lasers started firing, she immediately kicked hard towards the cube. It was as if this test had been designed for her, just as the first had been designed for her sister. Pulling with her arms and thrusting with her legs, she used the flow of the water to carry her directly to the power module. Reaching out, she grabbed hold of the edges of the cube and clung on. Was reaching the cube enough to pass the second test, or did she have to get inside it somehow? Her lungs were bursting! The next moment she felt her hands pass through the sides of the cube, as if it was dissolving, then her fingers closed around the power module. Immediately the water vanished as quickly as it had appeared, and she fell to the floor still clutching the glowing module. She was drenched and terrified, but at least she was alive. Nervously she looked up and watched to see if she had been in time to stop the lasers from activating. There was a moment of agonising silence then she smiled and let out a long sigh of relief. She had done it!

*

Princess Sekmet's craft appeared out of nowhere, close to Dagr's craft but without causing a disturbance in the water. Onboard, the prince studied the instruments in front of him carefully.

"Our crafts invisibility matrix has worked perfectly; the other craft has not detected our arrival. My scanners also detect that there are two people in the Nun structure, and one of them has the power module."

The princess stepped up next to him and pointed out of the window in the direction of the structure.

"We must stop them. If they are allowed to teleport back inside their craft they will get away, and we won't have the power to revive our Titans and Giants! Teleport me and a combat drone inside the structure immediately and then you launch an attack on Dagr's craft!"

Down in her craft's armoury there was a rack of combat drones. Automatically one bleeped into life and the locking mechanism on the rack sprang open. The drone floated free from the rack and moved into the centre of the room and then stopped and hovered motionless. Finally a beam of light came down from the ceiling and enveloped the drone; the next instant it had been teleported out of the craft.

Meanwhile the princess had prepared herself and stepped onto a glowing glass plate set into the floor of the control bridge. Turning to her brother she barked her commands. "Tell Hades to continue with the hypnotism of George; he must be converted to our cause before we get back to the Hollow Earth. Meanwhile attack Dagr's craft and destroy it!"

Then the princess vanished in a flash of light.

Keen to prove himself, the prince activated the weapons and manoeuvred the craft to a safe distance from Dagr's craft. As they were underwater, he selected a homing torpedo rather than any of their energy or laser weapons. Next a 3D image of the target appeared in front of him and with a finger he touched the place where he wanted the torpedo to hit. As soon as he did this, the weapon shot from the underside of his craft and cut through the water like a silver rocket. Seconds later it struck the Dagr's craft causing a blinding flash and billowing explosion of bubbles.

*

Hades continued to study his handy work on the boy. Oblivious to what the prince and princess were doing, he had continued his enhancement work on George. Now the enhancements were completed he was anxious to finish the hypnotherapy. He had transferred the boy into a different transparent tube, which hung vertically from the ceiling. This one was filled with pure oxygen and an anti-gravity vortex, which kept George floating in the centre of the tube. All around the tube were positioned an array of strobe lights which flickered on and off in rapid sequence. Hovering under the tube was a small pyramid shaped metal droid the size of a beach ball. The processing droid had dozens of tiny writhing plastic tentacles which were constantly reaching out and making adjustments to the strobe lighting system.

Hades looked on approvingly, as bit by bit the unconscious boys mind was being converted.

Chapter Ten

Deputy Commander Bridgid sat in the control bridge constantly monitoring the complicated array of 3D instruments which floated around her. She concentrated all her attention on what they were telling her was happening inside the underwater base. Lucy stood next to her, equally transfixed on the glowing instruments and the information they were displaying. Next to her stood the man wired into the navigation controls and floating behind him was the navigation robot, its different spheres glowing on and off. It was focused on keeping the craft in the correct position in the ocean.

"As soon as Commander Dagr gives the word I can teleport them back here," said Bridgid.

Lucy nodded; she was anxious to see her sister safely out of the base and back standing next to her as soon as possible.

Suddenly the whole craft shook violently, throwing her to the floor and sending Bridgid flying across the control bridge. Alarm sirens immediately began to wail loudly, forcing Lucy to cover her ears to minimise the pain.

"Were under attack!" shouted the Deputy. "It's the close proximity threat alarm that's deafening us." As soon as she could get up she sprinted across the floor and studied the alarm sensors. "The attacker is nearby but cloaked by an invisibility shield. Our scanners can't find them. It must be the prince and princess!"

The navigation robot and the pilot had also been thrown across the floor by the impact and were propped up against the far wall. The man was stunned, but managed to get up. However the robot was broken into several pieces, the spheres rolling about on the floor in different directions, no longer connected or glowing.

"Please can you shut that alarm off, it's so loud that I can't think straight!" shouted Lucy, as she staggered to her feet.

Without responding, Bridgid silenced the alarm and began to diagnose the damage to the craft. "The hull is still intact, but there is some internal damage to one of our hyper drive engines. Another blast like the first will cripple this craft if I don't act quickly!"

Lucy looked scared and felt the pit of her stomach tighten, while nightmare images flashed before her eyes. She remembered old war films she had seen on television, where submarines were hit by depth charges and the sailors drowned deep under water. They died horribly in the black depths of the cold dark ocean. She did not want that to happen to her. She did not want to die yet, not like this.

She was shaken out of her nightmare vision, by the shrill voice of Bridgid. "Our sensors have detected another missile which has just been fired at us. It will hit us in a few seconds!"

*

The first Dagr knew something was wrong was when Sekmet's combat drone teleported into the room and appeared opposite him. The square metal box immediately circled around him, at the same time slowly rotating so that Dagr could see its six different weapon pipes. It was showing off, deliberately trying to scare the commander into making a false move.

Dagr immediately activated his energy shield and its hazy blue light enveloped him like a dome, from head to the floor. Frustrated at not being able to get an easy shot, the combat drone circled around him even faster, using its scanners to test if the shield completely surrounded him. Realising that it did, the drone fired a laser burst at him from behind and then flew swiftly up over him to attack from the front.

*

Anne held up the power module in front of her with both hands and studied it closely. The four elemental crystals pulsated in sequence, casting eerie shadows across her face. However her wonderment was suddenly interrupted by a mysterious series of crackles over the communicator. Before she had time to respond the princess teleported into the inner sanctum, appearing directly in front of her.

Anne recoiled at the appearance of the woman and almost dropped the power module in surprise.

"That belongs to me!" shouted Sekmet in a commanding voice. "Give it to me now or I will destroy you!"

Anne stepped back and clutched the module close to her chest. "No way!"

The princess smiled gleefully "Good, your defiance means that I do not have to find an excuse to kill you!" Immediately she raised both hands and stretched them out in front of her, pointing in Anne's direction. Then Sekmet sneered at Anne as a double sonic blast echoed from her wrist weapons and hit the defenceless girl. The impact sent Anne sprawling across the floor like a rag doll, causing her to let go of the module.

Stunned, she looked up to see the princess striding towards her, with her wrist weapons still pointing at her, ready to fire the killer blasts.

*

"Emergency force field – immediate activation!" shouted Bridgid and the crafts automatic voice control hummed into life. Outside a flickering blue bubble of energy formed around the craft, just as the second torpedo slammed into it.

Inside, the closeness of the explosion shook the craft again, throwing Lucy across the bridge, to hit the far wall. "My arm! I think it's broken!" she shouted as she slumped to the floor in a heap.

Bridgid turned and looked at her then turned back and continued with her work on the controls. "I can't worry about you at the moment. I have to concentrate all my attention on protecting us from the next attack. The force field is only an emergency one and can only fend off a few more attacks!" Next she began to manipulate the controls and manoeuvre the craft to a position closer to the base; she hoped that whoever was firing at them would not risk hitting the base by accident. Even as she steered the craft to its new position a third torpedo suddenly appeared from a different direction and bore down on them.

"Hold on Lucy, the enemy has also changed position and have fired from a new direction. If I don't redirect our force field at full power to counter it, we will be blown to pieces!"

*

On the outside of the inner sanctum the commander suddenly squatted down low to avoid the attack of the combat drone and fired several laser blasts from both of his wrist controls. The wave length of the blasts allowed them to pass straight through his energy shield and struck the combat drone hard. To his amazement the blasts bounced right off the drone and hit the nearby walls causing a cascade of sparks. Before the drone could retaliate, he fired again using his weapons highest setting, but the blast bounced off again and the drone continued to hover in front of him completely untouched.

Fearful of what was going to happen, he checked his wrist control to make sure that his protective energy shield was at its maximum strength, and considered what to do next. Run and take cover? Teleport back to his own craft? What about Anne? What was happening to her? Was she under attack as well?

Before he could decide how to respond, the combat drone flew towards him and collided with his energy shield. Again to his amazement, the drone continued to do the unexpected and slowly began to force its way through the shield. Even as he stood transfixed, he saw it pushing its way towards him, like it was forcing its way through thick treacle. Using some unknown technology it was physically creating an opening in the shimmering blue wall of energy. In a confused response to the intrusion, he tried to step backwards, so that the shield would move back with him. He hoped to force the drone to start attacking the shield again. But it was too late. An instant later the drone was fully inside the shield and within reach. Before Dagr could shout, the drone extended a multi-bladed rotating weapon from the closest tube and slew him. The moment Dagr collapsed onto the floor, the energy shield vanished. Its mission now complete, the drone teleported back to its craft.

Chapter Eleven

Inside the inner sanctum, the princess towered over Anne like a praying mantis about to strike at its next meal. Then she paused for a moment and lowered her right hand. "You have already caused me a lot of problems, so a full sonic blast is too quick a death for you." With that, she fired a quick blast from her left wrist and stunned Anne again.

"That will paralyse you, long enough for me to escape with the power module and leave you to die in the explosion caused by the booby trap device I am going to leave behind. I don't merely want to take the power module; I want this entire base destroyed. And I want you trapped in here when it explodes."

With that she strode over to where the module lay on the floor and took a small black disc the size of a coin from her pocket and placed it onto the floor next to it.

"Despite its size, this disc bomb is extremely powerful. It will disrupt all the energy systems that are active in this base and cause them to overload and explode. You my dear will be reduced to atoms by the blast. Now all I've got to do is teleport out of here with the module. I've set the timer on my bomb for five of your minutes."

Next she bent down and picked up the power module, then with an arrogant swagger she approached Anne again. "Of course I could change my mind. It would still be more fun to blow you to bits myself, and then escape with the module."

With a cruel smile on her face, she raised her right arm and pointed its lethal wrist weapon at Anne.

*

The third torpedo exploded harmlessly against the emergency force field around Dagr's craft, but still sent shock waves through the length of it. Deputy Commander Bridgid struggled to keep the craft in position as the impact knocked it violently sideways. The impact also sent the injured Lucy rolling helplessly across the control bridge again.

"Can't you fire back at them? I can't take much more of this!" she shouted from her sprawling position on the floor.

"Negative; their invisibility shield is too good. And I can't lock on to the origin point of their torpedoes because they keep moving position after they have fired!"

Even as she spoke another torpedo came into range of their sensors and sped towards them.

Bridgid grimaced and held on to a nearby safety rail. "Brace for impact, I just hope that our force field holds again!"

*

The moment Princess Sekmet was about to fire the killer blast at Anne, the hologram of Dinvad appeared and caused a blinding light to fill the sanctum. Startled, the princess recoiled, shielding her eyes with her hands and stopping her from attacking Anne. In that moment she was distracted, the hologram floated across the room, hovered over Anne and teleported her and himself out of the inner sanctum.

After a few seconds the stars cleared from Sekmet's eyes, and she saw that Anne had vanished from the chamber. Cursing that she had been denied the opportunity to slay the girl, she quickly checked her explosive device was still on the floor and continuing to count down to detonation. Satisfied that there was only a few minutes left, she gripped the power module tightly and teleported out of the base and back to her own craft.

*

Outside the chamber, Anne materialised in midair and immediately fell to the floor. As she lay stunned the flickering hologram of Dinvad moved closer and stood guard over her. Trying to regain control of the situation, his electronically-projected mind scanned the room and quickly became aware that Dagr's lifeless body was on the other side of the chamber.

Realising that the man was beyond help, Dinvad leaned over Anne, trying to rouse her, his flat voice splurging out non-stop information. "I cannot heal you girl. I do not have that sort of technology on this base. Commander Dagr has been slain by one of the princess's combat drones. The base is about to explode. The only way you can survive is for your friends to teleport you back on board their craft and heal you."

By now Anne had begun to stir and was trying to raise herself onto one side. Unable to physically help her, Dinvad continued to talk.

"However Anne, I can give you something that will help you track your enemies and keep up with them."

He gestured with his hands and suddenly a small cube about the size of a matchbox materialised on the floor next to her. Through half-closed eyes she marvelled at its pure polished black surface and millions of pin-prick rainbow lights constantly flickering on it. Maybe it could help her to track the princess, but none of it would matter if she didn't get off this base now. If not, within seconds she would be blown to bits.

*

The moment the princess teleported back into her craft's control bridge, she immediately handed the power module to her brother. "Put this into a secure place at once!" Turning to the navigation robot she pointed at the control consoles. "We need to get away from here immediately. The timing device I left on that base is going to explode any moment!"

Keen to try and reassert his own authority the prince stepped up next to her. "What about Commander Dagr and the human girl?"

She immediately snapped back in annoyance at being interrupted by her brother. "The commander has been killed by my combat drone, and I wounded the girl. The blast will kill her and blow the base to atoms."

Having put her brother back in his place she returned her attention to escaping before the explosion. "Navigator do as I have ordered and get us out of here now!"

She suddenly felt the g-force against her body as her craft surged vertically away from the doomed underwater base.

On Dagr's craft, Deputy Commander Bridgid still battled to keep control.

"Finally, the attacks have stopped and my instruments have picked up a disturbance in the water close by. I think that our attacker is leaving us," she said. "Thankfully our force field held out against the impact of all those torpedoes."

"If they are leaving, does that mean they have already teleported into the base and got the power module from Anne and escaped?" stuttered Lucy anxiously. "We haven't heard anything from Dagr or Anne since the attacks began! Who knows what's been happening inside that base while we have been occupied with defending ourselves."

"You are probably right. As soon as I stabilise this craft I'll teleport into the base and find out what's happened," responded the woman firmly.

*

Deputy Bridgid appeared in the base's outer chamber in a flash of light and immediately saw the figure of Dagr sprawled on the floor. Sprinting across the room, she knelt down next to him and ran her fingertip scanner over his body, quickly establishing that he was dead. For a moment her face was pale with shock and then flushed with anger. Fighting to keep her emotions in check, she realised that Lucy had been correct and the enemy had teleported from their invisible craft into the base. Sekmet had tricked them! It was then that she heard a low groan and saw Anne slumped face down on the floor on the far side of the room.

She sprang up, dashed over to her and scanned the girl with the finger device. Anne was alive...just.

She turned her over and looked down at the school girl's battered and bruised face. "Who did this to you? Was it Sekmet? Did they get the power module?"

Anne managed to half open one eye and nod briefly, spluttering out words between coughs. "It was Princess Sekmet. She sent a combat drone to kill Dagr and she seized the module from me. We didn't stand a chance. Thankfully the holographic projection of Dinvad saved me. He gave me this cube to help us track where Sekmet's craft has gone."

Bridgid put her hand on the girl's brow to calm her. "Don't worry I will get a medical robot over here to help you as soon as I can."

Anne struggled to push herself up and shook her head. "No! We must get away from this base at once; the princess has planted a time bomb in the inner sanctum. It will blow us all to pieces if we don't go now!"

Bridgid looked grim. "Teleporting you like this may kill you, your injuries are too bad to withstand the molecular transformation!"

Anne angrily thrust her face directly in front of the woman's "We have no choice. Do it now!"

Bridgid nodded and immediately stood up. With a touch of her wrist control she and Anne vanished in a flash of light.

*

Back on the control bridge of Dagr's craft, Anne materialised onto the floor, next to Lucy. The younger one reached over and cuddled her motionless elder sister. They were both injured and terrified. Bridgid however forced herself to ignore them until she had got the craft to safety. She immediately saw that the pilot was dead.

He was slumped forward in his seat, the wires from his head snapped and torn out by the explosions. Having no time to be sad, she quickly positioned herself back into the middle of the floating controls and began to steer their craft away from the underwater base.

"If we are going to escape the explosion I will have to risk doing an uncontrolled power burst. It's the only way to get us far enough away from the base!"

Before Anne could respond, she felt the craft lurch upwards, like a cork exploding from a bottle of champagne. Despite the craft's g-force eliminators, she felt herself being pressed against the floor by the pressure. Would they survive?

Chapter Twelve

Anne awoke to find herself lying on a hospital-type bed, surrounded by humming instruments and mechanical arms which held medical equipment. The room was white and bright, and a spaghetti-like confusion of multi-coloured thin glowing tubes hung from the ceiling. She immediately sat up startled, not knowing where she was. The brightness of the room confused her and she opened and closed her eyes several times to focus her blurred vision.

"Don't worry sis, you're safe now and your injuries have been healed," said a familiar voice.

"Lucy? Thank goodness. Where are you? My eyes are still adjusting to this bright light."

In response, a blurred figure stepped out of the white background and approached Anne. Now she had someone to focus on, Anne's eyes rapidly adjusted to see her sister clearly. To her horror she saw a woman with green skin smiling down at her. The woman had short, dark green hair and her skin seemed to have tiny metallic specs inserted into the pale green flesh. Her eyes were a weird dark blue with pin prick black pupils in the centre.

"Who are you? How do you have my sister's voice? Where is Lucy? What have you done with her?"

The green woman leaned closer and gently held onto Anne's shoulders, stopping her from jumping off the bed. "It's me. I am your sister, Lucy. Look at my face, the colour may have changed, but my features are still the same!"

Anne stared in disbelief at the young woman and suddenly realised that it was her sister.

"What happened to you?"

Before responding, Lucy reached out and gripped a transparent chair which was floating close to the bed and sat down on it. Then she reached out and held Anne's hands tightly. "We were both close to death. The only way for Bridgid to save us was to give us a temporary genetic enhancement. In other words stimulate our Atlantis DNA to heal us super quickly. It's given me temporary powers which have increased my analytical abilities, but the temporary side effect is also to change the pigment of my skin and hair. My eyes have also been modified temporarily. Don't worry, the physical changes and powers will only last a few hours."

Anne chuckled. "In other words you've been changed from a swot into a super-swot!" Then as soon as the joke passed, Anne suddenly frowned as an alarming thought occurred to her. "If that was a side effect of their technology healing you, what was the side effect of them healing me? Am I green as well?"

"Definitely not," responded her sister, and she leaned across Anne towards a white table and picked up a foil thin hand mirror. Without saying another word she passed her the mirror. Anne hesitated for a moment, hoping that she did not have any of the weird side effects that her sister had. Taking a deep breath to prepare herself, she held it up to see her face. What she saw made her gasp out loud.

"I'm blue! My face is blue! My hair is blue and my eyes are blue as well!"

Lucy giggled playfully. "It's not just your face. You're blue all over. Just like I'm green all over."

Now alert and wide awake Anne slid off the bed and tried to stand up. She was still wearing the pressure suit Dagr had given her and took a moment to steady herself. With her right index finger she pulled open the neck of her suit and looked down inside. She gave a long loud sigh as she saw that she was indeed blue all over.

Lucy stood up and stepped next to her. "Now you have recovered, we need to report to Bridgid and get an update on what's going on."

*

Bridgid was in the control bridge waiting for them. As soon as they entered, she beckoned them over to stand each side of her and then directed her attention to Anne.

"We have no time to waste, so I will update you while we are in-flight. A lot has happened while you were in your induced coma. Firstly, Commander Dagr is dead. He was slain by Sekmet's combat drone. Secondly, as Lucy has by now told you, a temporary side effect of your cure is not just the blue skin, but you now have a short term ability. Your power has enhanced your natural strength and athletic abilities."

Anne stood shocked. She realised that her body felt better that ever, but had assumed that it was just another side effect of the treatment.

"You will both have an opportunity to test your powers when we get inside Sekmet's secret underground base. Thirdly, we are now in a high Earth orbit and still hidden from any human radar devices. Sadly our own tracking equipment has been destroyed, so we cannot follow Sekmet back to her secret base."

Bridgid pointed at the broken tracking equipment and indicated where she had tried to connect Dinvad's cube to the crafts equipment with cables. The cube looked dull and lifeless.

"I was hoping that the cube would help us. Unfortunately no matter what I try, it refuses to integrate itself into our ship's guidance system."

Instinctively Anne stepped forward and touched it with both hands. "Dinvad said that I would be able to operate it. Let me concentrate for a moment and see if I can connect to it."

As soon as she closed her eyes, the strange black cube glowed with a weird green light and made electrical crackling sounds. Without warning there was a loud hiss and a beam of light projected from the cube. A moment later the light formed into a human figure. Then the light blended its colours and formed into the body of a young boy. He was quite tall and thin with a full head of fair hair, which was cut short and angular. He wore dark overalls, which were edged in gold and silver. His boots were ankle-length and metallic.

"I am a holographic memory projection of Jaxar, agent supreme of Atlantis. I was twelve years old when Dinvad created this projection of me. It was made at the same time that he made a memory projection of himself. I was only to be activated in the case of extreme emergency."

Anne let go of the cube and stepped cautiously towards the flickering image of the boy. "Dinvad gave you to me to control. Are you connected into this craft's tracking system and can you read the ship's database to understand what is happening and why we need your help?"

The boy looked away for a moment and concentrated. "Yes I am. I can now track Sekmet's craft and I know where it has gone. I can also pilot this craft, better than any other pilot. I am also aware of what Sekmet and her brother are planning and why you are trying to stop them."

Nearby, Lucy pulled an impressed face. "That's certainly saved us all a lot of time discussing things."

Anne stepped up close to Jaxar. "Now that's all settled, take us to where Sekmet has got George."

The flickering boy nodded and smiled. "Changing course as we speak. The entrance to the princess's Hollow Earth secret base is now locked into this craft's flight controls. Here we go!"

Suddenly they all felt the craft bank to the right and speed up as it plummeted through the Earth's atmosphere.

*

Sekmet's craft swept across the icy wastes of Antarctica at breathtaking speed, dropping so low that it scattered clouds of ice and snow behind it. Ahead of it towered the imposing volcanic dome of Mount Erebus. Abruptly the craft flipped skywards and followed the steep sides of the ice bound mountain until it reached the summit, then levelled off and stopped dead.

There were two craters on the summit; the smaller, side one was dormant, however the much larger main crater contained an active lava lake, one of the few permanent lava lakes on the Earth. After hovering motionless for a moment the craft descended vertically towards the bubbling lava. The craft descended to the point where it was going to touch the lava, and then the liquid parted as if pushed aside by an invisible force. The craft continued to descend untouched by the white hot lava until it disappeared from sight and the lava closed over it.

Inside the ship, Sekmet stood next to the pilot and her brother. A fully hypnotised and conditioned George stood next to Hades. The boy was dressed in a silver and black pressure suit with belt and metal head band. This band had a row of coloured lights which blinked randomly. However his body had changed as a result of the procedures that Hades had performed on him. He was several inches taller and his forehead was larger, because his brain inside had expanded. There was a strange vacant look in his eyes, as if his thoughts were far away. Confident that George was now on her side, the princess continued to talk as the craft descended through the boiling, fiery liquid outside.

"The force field around our craft keeps us safe from the lava. The auto pilot knows the access codes and can get us safely past all our inner defences and back inside the Hollow Earth."

Next the craft stopped descending and began to travel sideways through the lava.

"We are about to go through the second barrier. Our craft's polarity will instantly reverse to match the barrier's force field so we get through the massive air lock into the chamber while the molten lava is held back."

Close to the craft, the vast circular air lock slid aside, but the wall of lava was held back by the invisible force field. Next the lava parted just as it had on the surface and the craft emerged unmarked from it and entered the pressurised chamber. Then the metal doors of the air lock closed again with a loud clang. The chamber was pitch black, but as soon as the craft entered it, a large glowing light set in the roof came to life. In the weird green light, the polished walls of the chamber became visible. Looking through the craft's viewing port they could all see that at the far end of the chamber was the wide entrance to a dark tunnel.

"Now we fly down the access shaft. This is our third line of security. The walls of the shaft are lined with combat drones. Without transmitting the correct codes they will attack whoever enters the shaft."

As they sped down the shaft they passed weird metallic rock-like formations which seemed to be growing from the shaft's walls. They looked like pointed metal columns of crystal, entwined with segmented cables and flashing lights.

For several minutes they continued to hurtle down the tubular shaft at breathtaking speed, then suddenly stopped. The end of the shaft was blocked by a closed metal iris. The stop was so abrupt that they all lurched forward in the control bridge of the craft. Sekmet composed herself and continued.

"The final code allows us access into the Hollow Earth complex. This code is changed on a random basis. Without it we cannot open it."

After a moment the large metal segments of the iris slid open with a grinding sound and then the craft flew through. Immediately the iris closed behind it with a loud clang.

Now the craft was in a wide tunnel, lined with jagged crystal growths on all sides. Expertly piloted, the craft twisted its way between them and vanished into the darkness.

Chapter Thirteen

Bridgid's craft rapidly descended over the main crater of Mount Erebus, only halting its vertical descent just feet above the bubbling lava.

On board, the image of Jaxar spoke to the others in steady automated tones. "In order to follow Sekmet I need to complete a set series of procedures. Step one. I have to reverse the polarity of this craft's force field. That will allow us to travel through the lava without being harmed."

Anne frowned, her blue skin wrinkling tightly. "How do you know all this Jaxar?"

The image of the long dead boy turned to face her. "Dinvad was the high scientist of Atlantis. He was the person who developed all their security systems and defences, including its remote outposts across the world and the entrances to the Hollow Earth."

Able to multitask, Jaxar continued to talk to Anne at the same time as he controlled the craft. Even as he addressed all those in the control bridge, the craft suddenly dropped quickly and the lava parted to allow it through and then cover it.

Jaxar continued. "Next I need to steer us horizontally through the lava and into a side chamber. Once again I need to get the force field polarity correct and all the access codes correct. Firstly, to hold back the lava and then to open and close the air lock. It is unlikely they have changed the codes from when Dinvad programmed them ten thousand years ago. There would be no reason for Sekmet to do that, if she thinks that we have all been destroyed."

A moment later the ship emerged from the lava into a pressurised chamber and came to a halt, hovering silently as the huge air lock closed behind them. Meanwhile Jaxar prepared to fly through the next set of defences.

"Now I have to steer us down the access shaft. This is the Hollow Earth's third line of security. The walls of the shaft are lined with combat drones. Without transmitting the correct codes they will attack us."

Lucy anxiously turned to Bridgid. "What happens if these ancient codes no longer work?"

The woman tried to hide the worried tone in her voice. "Let's hope that they do work."

Without responding to either, Jaxar moved the craft forward and it started to fly down the shaft. "Transmitting access code now. Let's hope that they have not been changed since Sekmet and Cronus came out of suspended animation!"

After a few minutes of steep descent the holographic boy showed his first sign of panic. "I am detecting multiple power surges along the walls of the shaft. The drones are activating!"

Bridgid stepped forward to be close to Jaxar. "Are they simply activating as part of some automatic response to receiving a code after such a long time? Ten thousand years is a long time for drones to be dormant!"

Jaxar shook his head. "No. Sekmet's craft will have had to use codes to get out and back in again. They must have changed the codes!"

As they sped down the shaft they passed the weird metallic rock-like formations which were growing from the shaft's walls. The pointed metal columns of crystal, entwined with segmented cables and flashing lights, suddenly began to move. Then from the end of each column dozens of combat drones separated and floated free.

"The drones are coming alive! We are about to be attacked!"

*

Meanwhile Sekmet's craft entered the Hollow Earth's landing area through an opened metal iris, and stopped to hover over a large circular platform. The platform was attached to a tubular walkway which led into a domed building, which jutted out the rock face of the huge cavern. There was an identical platform and walkway on the other side of the building. Under the landing area was a lake of bubbling lava. The landing area extended from the side of the cavern wall and was supported by thick metal struts. The lava lake below was prevented from rising to engulf it; by a glowing force field.

Sekmet's craft descended silently and landed on its designated platform.

Standing in the control bridge she gave her orders to the others. "Hades, take the boy with you to the Central Administration Laboratory and get to work on bringing the Giants and Titans to life. Cronus, you secure this craft in its re-charging connector and then join me in the base's Command Centre with the power module."

*

George was aware of what was happening but found that he was not able to control his actions. It was as if his head was inside another body, like a helpless passenger trapped inside an airplane which was locked on auto pilot.

The Central Administration Laboratory (CAL) was the main experimental area and was next to the Command Centre. They were linked by a series of full length sliding doors. The CAL was a square room with metal walls and floor. The ceiling was made of roughly cut rock and had lots of coloured cables clipped into it, criss-crossing it like a trawler net. There were a series of control consoles set into free standing tables in the centre of the CAL. One wall had a series of large glass panels which allowed the occupants to look into an adjoining chamber. This was called the Containment Chamber and was brightly lit and looked like a storage area, with walls lined with metal racks. However dozens of glass cylinders hung from the ceiling like the ones George and his sisters had been imprisoned in when on the spacecraft. They were suspended from individual frames which looked as if they could be lowered. George also noted that there were a series of metal grills set into the floor of the chamber.

Looking in the other direction George saw Sekmet and Cronus entering the adjoining Command Centre. This was a large spherical metal room with glittering walls. In the centre was a raised crystal pillar on which hovered a glowing ball. This was a perfect replica of what the surface of the Earth looked like ten thousand years ago. On it was marked where Atlantis had been and all the hidden bases around the world. The flat floor of the Command Centre was made of alternate rings of metal and strong glass. Through these glass sections George could see that there was a lake of molten lava far below, which was held in place by layers of invisible force fields. In front of the crystal pillar there was a raised metallic dais on which there was a complex electronic frame, designed to hold something. Then George realised what it was for, as he saw Princess Sekmet place the new power module into it. As soon as it slotted into place, the whole area was filled with a blinding glow and the boy had to shield his eyes for a moment. Finally the glow faded and he could see that the metal dais was crackling with electricity as the power module energised the equipment.

The princess turned on her heels and faced George and Hades, staring at them through the sliding glass doors. "The power module is fully integrated into the system. Now get to work and revive those Giants and Titans!"

Chapter Fourteen

Jaxar's image floated across the floor of Bridgid's control bridge and positioned itself into the pilot's manual control seat.

"Hold on I am going to have to fly this myself. There is no way that this craft's automatic flight controls will be able to outmanoeuvre or fight these combat drones!"

Anne gripped onto a nearby hand rail, sensing what was about to happen "How can we fight them?"

Jaxar responded without turning around. "We can fight back because I am bringing this craft's weapons on-line now!"

Meanwhile outside in the shaft, multiple drones detached themselves from the ends of the metallic columns and began to buzz around like angry bees bursting from a hive. In response, the craft accelerated through the twisting swarm, scattering them. As if suddenly realising that it was their target, the swarm swept along after the craft.

"I can't let them overtake us. If they surround us in mid-flight they will blast us to pieces in a laser cross-fire!" exclaimed Jaxar loudly, as if he was now alive and not just an electronic memory.

"This craft has four sonic charges, normally used for planet surveys and prospecting. I will fire them behind us in a wide pattern. I want to destroy the closest twenty drones and collapse some of the shaft roof on to the others."

"Isn't there a danger that we might be caught in the blasts?" said Lucy as she calculated the risks at super speed with her enhanced mind.

"Yes," responded Jaxar without emotion. "But as it's me who is the pilot, our chances of survival are good. Better than any automation or human pilot would give us."

On his command the four sonic charges ejected from the underside of the craft and separated to block the way for the pursuing drones.

"The timing of the detonations has to be staggered by half a second each, to guarantee destroying the maximum number of drones."

On command the four oil drum sized sonic charges exploded, filling the shaft behind the craft with blinding light and ear splitting noise. The blast of destructive sound ripped back up the shaft towards the drones, blowing the leaders to pieces. Dozens exploded in all directions, scattering flames and fragments of debris.

"My sensors tell me that I just destroyed twenty-eight drones. Better than I expected, unfortunately the walls are still intact."

Jaxar studied the sensors in silence for a moment. "There are still 47 drones chasing us. Now they are taking up a wide formation, to prevent me destroying so many next time."

"Next time? But you don't have any more sonic charges," gasped Anne.

"We know that, but the drones don't. They will hold off from attacking us for a few minutes. That will buy me time to calculate a laser blast pattern to destroy some more and hold off the rest."

Even as he spoke the closest of the drones spread into a formation and began to overtake the craft on two sides.

The craft fired first, spitting out lines of red energy in several directions at once and the nearest drones exploded into flaming fragments. The craft fired again and several more drones exploded.

However another wave of them converged on the craft from above, this time firing first. Green lines of laser energy spat from them and criss-crossed around the craft, narrowly missing it.

"I can only dodge their attacks for a few more minutes. We need to escape through the next security barrier quickly!" announced Jaxar.

"What barrier and when do we get there!" exclaimed Anne, gripping the hand rail even tighter.

"It's an ultra-strong access iris, which opens and lets us fly through to the next section of the Hollow Earth," responded Jaxar without turning around.

"How do you get the iris to open and close?" questioned Lucy, her enhanced brain seeking how to overcome any problem.

"I have the access codes," responded Jaxar.

"Are these codes going to work this time?" pressed Lucy.

"We won't know until we get to the iris."

"How soon do we get there?" interrupted Anne.

Jaxar studied the instruments again. "Two minutes."

Outside, more of the drones detached themselves from the walls of the shaft and swarmed after the craft. No longer deterred, they all began to open fire on it, filling the shaft with laser bursts and bouncing sparks.

Jaxar felt the craft shudder from the impact of the blasts. The shaft was getting narrower and the drones getting closer. No matter how much he swerved the craft and tried to dodge the attackers, he was running out of time...

Suddenly the closed metal iris came into view.
"Sending access codes now!"

*

George stood next to Hades as the little man manipulated the controls within the Central Administration Laboratory. They both stood looking through the large glass viewing window into the Containment Chamber. Behind them the prince and princess strode into the CAL from the adjoining Command Centre.

Sekmet spoke first. "The power module is operating at peak performance. We have more than enough energy to carry out our plans. Hades, connect the boy to the instruments and begin the first procedure."

In response Hades took hold of George's arms and guided him forward and stood him in front of the main controls, next to a large viewing window. Next he pulled several wires from the control console and connected them to the boy's head with tiny circular stickers. He then began to wave his hands over the flickering controls. "George, I want you to concentrate your thoughts on one of the test subjects in the containment chamber. With your mind, select one of the tubes you see hanging in front of you. Now focus on the embryo inside and bring it to life."

George still felt like he was in a daze, but found himself having to comply with Hades instructions. Instinctively he closed his eyes and concentrated all his efforts onto one of the large tubes hanging from a frame in the chamber.

At the back of his mind he still thought that this was all a nightmare, or worse still if it was real; then his captors had made a mistake and he had no power to bring all these monsters back from the dead. Beads of sweat began to form on his forehead and his hands began to tremble slightly. Suddenly he took a sharp breath and opened his eyes. To his amazement the tube he was concentrating on began to wobble slightly. Automatically the frame holding it lowered the tube into position and held it over one of the drainage grills set into the floor.

With a whooshing sound the bottom of the tube swung open and the green contents splashed onto the floor. Wide-eyed, George watched transfixed as the slimy liquid seeped into the drains and left a wet body lying on the floor.

Hades shouted at George again. "Concentrate harder, boy. Get it to stand up. Use your power to bring it back to life!"

George suddenly felt excited that he had such power. On the surface world he was just an ordinary schoolboy, but down here he was someone special. Encouraged by his success he concentrated on the prone figure and willed it to stand up. After a moment the figure began to move, stretching and moving like someone waking up from a deep sleep. The more George focused his thoughts, the more he found he could get the figure to move the way he wanted. It was like having a puppet he could control without using strings!

Observing what was happening, the prince and princess looked on very satisfied. The boy was performing even better than they could imagine. Within hours they would have him reviving the largest and most terrible Giants and Titans.

Suddenly Sekmet's personal wrist alarm sounded and she discreetly stepped back from the others to see what the problem was. As soon as she saw what the warning was about she whispered to her brother. "The security systems have detected Dagr's spacecraft in the main access shaft. Our combat drones are attacking it now, but if it gets through the inner iris we need to stop it before it gets any further. Despatch more combat drones to intercept the craft and destroy it!"

Chapter Fifteen

Bridgid's spacecraft was about to smash into the big metal iris, when it began to slide open. The access codes had worked!

Twisting and turning the craft to avoid the cross fire from the drones, Jaxar decided to take a gamble.

He needed to close the iris behind them, before any of the drones could follow their craft through. He needed to shoot down the nearest drones, allowing the craft to get far enough ahead of the rest of the swarm, so it could get through the iris and issue the closure security codes. He hoped the iris would close fast enough, before any of the drones could get through.

Anxious, he voiced his concerns out loud. "Our lasers are almost out of power. I can only fire one more volley. The target selection will have to be precise because the drones are constantly shifting position!"

Then Jaxar's head began to glow and lines of light extended from it into the craft's controls.

"Hold tight!"

Immediately the craft twisted and turned wildly, darting in and out of the closest drones like a bat hunting its prey. Then multiple lasers lashed out from it and blasted them, filling the shaft with blinding light. Out of the flaming inferno and confusion, Bridgid's craft flew through the open iris like a blur.

"Closure code being transmitted now!" shouted the hologram.

Seconds later the huge iris slid shut behind the craft and dozens of the pursuing drones smashed into the metal barrier, filling the shaft with billowing flames and the deafening noise of explosions. Even on the safe side of the iris, the crew of Bridgid's craft felt the vibrations of the explosions.

"We made it!" shouted the hologram.

"You did it, you saved us Jaxar!" whooped Anne punching the air with her fist.

Looking ahead through the viewing port, she saw that they had emerged into a vast cavern lined with giant glittering stalactites and stalagmites. Areas of the ceiling were illuminated by a strange green glow which came from patches of fungus. The floor of the cavern was littered with glittering crystals of different shapes and sizes. Directly ahead, the cavern separated into several smaller tunnels, each one lit by rows of lights set into the roof.

Jaxar brought the craft to a halt and got it to hover motionless while he accessed the electronic map Dinvad had embedded into his memory thousands of years ago.

"Now where do we go?" said Bridgid striding across the control bridge and positioning herself behind Jaxar's flickering image.

"We continue through this cavern and follow Dinvad's mind map. That will guide us down the correct tunnel to the Hollow Earth base. Then we can land in secret and get inside".

Without warning one of the giant stalactites directly above the hovering craft glowed brightly and then split away from cavern's ceiling. Like a guided weapon it fell silently, its metal-tipped point glinting in the green glow. A moment later it smashed into the roof of the hovering craft, its point penetrating all the way through the hull and out the bottom. Punctured dead centre, the craft crashed to the floor, the point of the stalactite embedding itself into the ground. The noise of the crash echoed throughout the cavern for several minutes, like the clashing of giant symbols. Finally the cavern fell silent, and the craft lay pinned to the crystal scattered floor, smoke billowing from under its rim on one side.

Stunned, Jaxar quickly studied his memory circuits. "That was a new defence weapon! It must have been installed after Dinvad designed the other security systems!"

Before anyone could respond, there was an explosion in the engine room. "We must evacuate!" ordered Bridgid, and she reached out and operated the controls to the emergency escape doors.

"She is correct" added Jaxar "This craft is beyond repair and the stalactite weapon will be linked into the main alarm system of the Hollow Earth. Cronus and Sekmet will have been automatically warned of our arrival. Do as the commander says; you need to evacuate as soon as possible!"

"What about you Jaxar?" retorted Anne as she grabbed hold of Lucy and pulled her towards the open door at the rear of the control bridge.

"I will stay on board and defend this craft for as long as possible. That way Cronus and Sekmet will believe you are all still on board. They will destroy this craft and believe that you have all been killed. That way you can continue your mission without being detected."

Anne shook her head in disagreement. "But what about you Jaxar? The memory cube Dinvad gave me will be destroyed. You will no longer exist."

The flickering image of the young boy turned and looked back at her, his face grim but determined; almost as if he was alive. "Get out now! My sensors have detected a squad of drones flying up from Sekmat's base! They are on their way through the lower tunnels to destroy us!"

Realising that she had no choice, she turned and fled hand in hand with her sister.

Bridgid, Anne and Lucy ran down a flight of metal stairs, because the power to the internal transporter had failed when the craft crashed. Coughing and spluttering they forced their way through the thick black smoke which was filling the corridors. "We need to get into our jet pack harnesses!" shouted Bridgid over the noise of explosions. "It's the only way we can get far enough from this spacecraft before the combat drones arrive!"

Bridgid yanked open a locker and pulled out a strange looking device. It was like a small back pack made from hard shiny metal with black straps. At the base of it was a small metal gyroscope and two small directional fins. Anne and Lucy watched how she pulled hers on and fastened it in place. They then picked up one each and quickly copied her, pulling them on tight.

"These are magnetic back packs. They are only to be used in emergencies and are designed to fly the wearer a short distance."

Next she pressed a control on her wrist and a panel in the metallic wall of the craft slid loudly to one side. The door was about six feet above the rocky ground and one at a time the trio jumped out. All around them black smoke billowed and twisted like a living thing. Anne wiped the tears from her eyes because the smoke stung them, meanwhile Lucy covered her nose and mouth with her hands to stop the stinging at the back of her throat.

"Follow me over there. We must hide behind those crystal pillars!" ordered Bridgid.

The trio sprinted across the weird sparkling ground and threw themselves behind a ten foot high pillar of glittering quartz. Luckily it was so wide that they could all crouch behind it without being seen.

Ten drones suddenly flew into view from the closest tunnel and began to circle around the craft like a swarm of bees. Anne watched as they stopped and hovered in midair as if choosing individual attack positions. And then the attack began. Blinding light and deafening sound filled the cavern. The noise and flashes were so bad that Anne and the others had to cover their ears and turn away from the explosions.

On board the beleaguered craft, the hologram of Jaxar, worked frantically to fight off the attack. Shot for shot, blast for blast he countered every assault, as flames and explosions filled the control bridge. Even though he had merged his memory with the craft's weapons he ignored the inevitable destruction that was soon to engulf him and focused all his efforts on destroying as many drones as possible. He knew that he needed to keep the full attention of every drone on him, so Anne and the others could escape without being seen. Abruptly the craft was rocked by more explosions and Jaxar realised that all its weapons and defence systems had failed. He and the craft were now helpless.

As if sensing this, the drones began to change position and set up a cross fire to blast the craft from different angles. Billowing smoke spewed out of the craft where the hull was struck again by the energy blasts. Without warning the drones pulled away and fired simultaneous blasts at the helpless craft. Instantly it was ripped apart by a single deafening explosion.

Anne cringed as the noise and shock wave struck her and shattered the crystal column next to her. At the same moment Lucy stifled a scream, covered her ears and buried her head in the rubble strewn floor. Instinctively

Bridgid pushed Anne onto the ground alongside her sister and threw herself across them both, to protect them from the falling rubble and fragments of metal from the destroyed craft.

They lay there for several minutes, keeping deliberately quiet and motionless as a film of dust settled over them and the surrounding cavern.

Then taking a risk, Bridgid whispered to them through clenched teeth; sounding like a serpent's hiss. "Don't move or speak until the drones have gone. They are certain to scan the wreckage to see if there were any survivors from the craft!"

Even as she spoke, several of the drones swept slowly through the cavern, scanning the few remaining pieces of wreckage and the large crater at the centre of the explosion-blasted ground. They hummed and whined for a moment, some scanning with search lights as they flew across the rubble strewn floor. And then as quickly as they had entered the cavern, the drones left.

Once Bridgid was certain that they had gone, she sprang to her feet and then pulled the others up by their collars.

"We need to get away from here as quickly as possible. Jaxar did well to keep them occupied for as long as he did. But he was destroyed and we need to go before those drones return!"

Bridgid quietly took several items from the small pouches attached to the side of her back pack and held them out.

"We each have a locator-tracker. These will guide us to the centre of the Hollow Earth base. And hopefully to George. It will also help me to find a place to plant some time bombs to destroy the base, once we have escaped."

"Bombs?" gasped Anne.

In response the commander tapped her back pack. "Yes, I have a selection of timed explosive devices; small but extremely powerful."

Meanwhile Lucy looked across the expanse of the cavern and saw what lay ahead. "There are five tunnels leading off from this cavern. "Which one do we go down?"

"We increase our chances of success if we separate," responded Bridgid.

"Separate!" gasped Lucy anxiously.

"She's right," said Anne. "That way at least one of us has a chance of finding George."

Bridgid looked at her tracking device; it was the size of a matchbox and pulsated with inner light. It glowed brighter in the direction you had to travel. "All five tunnels lead in the direction of the centre of the Hollow Earth but by different routes. Take your pick."

The tunnels were hundreds of yards away, across a battle scarred floor, covered in razor sharp shards of shattered crystal. Following Bridgid's instructions, Anne nervously activated her jet pack and felt it throbbing into life.

The commander quickly activated hers and pulled out the hand controls, showing the two girls how to adjust the power, speed and direction of the device. "Follow my lead across the cavern, then as we reach the tunnels, split off and take the one you want. I am going to go into the middle one."

Then without paying them any more attention, she brought her jet pack to life, floated about ten feet into the air and then sped off across the cavern. Anne marvelled at how such a device could operate silently. Lucy was also amazed at the technology, guessing that the device used some sort of electromagnetic repelling principles.

Next Anne took firm grip of her hand controls and increased the power on her own device and felt her feet lift off from the ground. It was an amazing feeling, to float silently without effort. Gaining confidence with the details of the controls, she rose higher into the air and rotated to face the direction Bridgid had taken. "Come on sis, follow me!"

Lucy had watched what the others had done and was confident enough to start her device and rise straight into a high position and follow Anne. Although she was more interested in the science behind the technology, she too was excited at being able to silently fly.

Chapter Sixteen

"The intruder has been destroyed by the combat drones!" shouted Cronus triumphantly, keen to impress his sister as he returned to the Command Centre with a spring in his step.

"Good," she responded, "but I am still curious as to how Dagr's craft survived the explosion in the Bermuda Triangle. Never mind, that's something we will never know."

Meanwhile in the Central Administration Laboratory, George was enjoying his new found ability to control other beings. The figure in the containment area slowly finished standing up like a drunken man, uncertain of its ability to balance correctly. George looked on with an open mouth as the human shape straightened itself and the last of the slime slowly slid off and oozed over the floor. The figure was seven feet tall, powerful and muscular. Its skin was mottled brown and black with scaly lizard-like qualities. But what shocked George the most was the creature's head. It had a normal face but only had one large red eye set into the middle of its forehead.

"It's a Cyclops! A creature from Greek mythology!"

Standing behind George, Hades nodded with approval at the boy's knowledge. "Our main army is made up of thousands of battle trained Cyclops troops. Once we have fully tested your powers on several of these, you will start on the larger Titans and Giants."

George felt himself getting swept along by the excitement of being able to control an army of mythical monsters. Sensing this, Hades moved closer to the boy. "Now test the creature. See if you have full control of it."

George concentrated again and the Cyclops became more animated, walking up and down and stretching its arms above its head, like a person who had just woken up and got out of bed. Next he got it to do lots of exercises, jumps and movements to test that it was fully mobile and ready to fight. George felt excited that he had such power over such a awesome creature.

George turned to Hades and felt confident enough to question the tiny man.

"If you were alive before Atlantis exploded and sank, what was it like?"

Hades narrowed his bulging green eyes for a moment and then responded, confident that the boy was now on his side.

"It had hundreds of towers made of crystal and metal, which reached high into the sky. Floating buildings that hovered over the main city. Vast underground travel tubes connecting all parts of the island-continent to the main city. And of course the Zodiac crystals powered it all."

"And what about the people who lived there?" enquired George.

"We were an advanced high-tech race; while the humans on the mainland were backward barbarians. It was us who gave knowledge to the ancient Egyptians, Britons and Chinese."

Keen to focus George back onto controlling the Cyclops, Hades urged the boy on.

"Excellent boy!" exclaimed Hades. "Now let's revive another Cyclops!"

*

Anne steered away from the other two and flew into her choice of tunnels. As soon as she was alone, her exhilaration at flying was replaced by the feelings of fear and loneliness. Only now did it strike her how desperate her situation was. Trapped miles underground without her parents, teachers or friends knowing where she was. What was happening to her brother? Would Lucy survive? Would they all end their days down here?

Now the walls of the tunnel began to close in on her. The light from the cavern had become a distant glow behind her and now she was surrounded by darkness. She brought her jet pack to an abrupt halt and hovered in the air, fearing that she would crash into a wall. What now?

Trying to keep calm she looked in the direction which she had been travelling and noticed a faint red light in the distance. Hoping that it was a way out, she manoeuvred the jet pack slowly forward. For what seemed like ages she flew steadily, and the light seemed to remain tantalisingly far off. Then unexpectedly she had arrived and the light flared brightly in front of her.

It was a dead end. She was faced with a circular metal air lock set into the rock wall at floor level. It was little more than a crawl space. How was she supposed to get in? Bridgid had not left her with any lock-pick technology. As if in answer, the heavy metal door slid aside. Anne guessed that there was a motion sensor close by and set to allow automatic access. Clearly the people of ancient Atlantis did not believe anyone who did not have proper security clearance could get this far. Their over confidence could be their weakness, she thought.

She also realised that she could not get through the narrow entrance with her back pack on. With a loud sigh of disappointment she landed, took the device off and placed it carefully on the floor. She had no idea if she would come back this way and need it again. Then she got down onto the floor and crawled through the metal rimmed entrance. No sooner had she emerged on the other side, than the air lock closed behind her with a clang.

On the other side of the air lock was a larger passage which she could stand up in. All the walls, floor and ceiling were made of a dull grey metal. Artificial light flooded in from ceiling panels every few yards. She guessed that she was in some sort of access tunnel or air shaft. The passage led in one direction, towards the distant hum of machinery. Wiping the sweat from her blue-skinned brow, she strode in the direction of the hum.

*

Meanwhile, Lucy had come to an identical air lock, taken off her back pack and crawled through. The air lock slammed shut behind her. Standing up in the passage she had a choice of directions. The air lock had led her to a junction where three passages met. The one on the left was only dimly lit, the one in the middle was lined with lots of metal pipes which were leaking hissing steam and the one on the right was like a normal rectangular corridor.

Unsure what to do, she pulled out her tracking device and studied it. The side facing up had a very simple screen with a red direction arrow to follow. It pointed down the passage on the right.

Beads of sweat formed on her green brow and nervously she set off down the silent passage, the clunk of her boots echoing around her.

*

Bridgid came to a large person-sized air lock shaped like an iris. Unlike the larger ones they had flown the spacecraft through, this one was made of crystal rather than metal. Expertly she landed, removed her back pack and propped it up against the tunnel wall. Next she took out her tracker to confirm that she needed to get to the other side of the iris. Then she put it away and took out her electronic lock de-coder, which was a similar looking flickering device the size of a matchbox. This was programmed with all the security codes used by ancient Atlantis and she hoped that the prince and princess were so overconfident that they had not bothered to change them.

The de-coder bleeped and the iris spiralled open to reveal a brightly lit interior. Confidently she stepped through and the door closed behind her.

The passage inside only led in one direction and was so narrow that people could only walk in single file. The walls and ceiling glowed with a strange white light, and the grooved floor glowed green. Focused on the mission, she paused to check that she still had the bombs she needed, then strode off. The passage started to slope steadily downwards and she guessed that there would be more obstacles to overcome than just locked doors.

*

Anne had been walking down the passage at a brisk pace, her newfound strength giving her a noticeable spring in her step. Nor was she out of breath. She was enjoying her enhanced energy; even if it was only temporary. It was the blue skin she was not so keen on.

Then the passage split into two taller, narrower tunnels. Stopping, she peered into the one on the left. It had a narrow line of lights set into the ceiling which enabled her to see that there was no floor in the tunnel for thirty feet. Stepping to the edge she peered down into what looked like a bottomless pit shrouded in blackness. She did not know if it was a trap or simply the way the underground city was constructed; but there was no way she could jump the length of the pit. Looking up she noticed that there was a narrow pipe running along the length of the ceiling. Looking closer she saw that it was held in place at regular intervals by sturdy support brackets. She concluded that the pipe would be able to hold her weight.

Before she committed herself to make the jump, she back tracked to the tunnel on the right and peered into it. By contrast it was a white walled box about twenty feet long. Out of its walls extended lots of inch thick tubes, blocking the way. They looked solid and part of some complex machine. She guessed the tunnel was an access way which allowed people to carry out maintenance. Some of the tubes looked permanent, while others which blocked the way retracted into the wall for a few seconds and then came out again. Anne could not see how anyone could get through to the normal tunnel on the other side. Realising that she would have to take the other tunnel, she stretched her arms above her head to flex her muscles. Positioning herself in the left tunnel, she took several paces back as if she was about to do the long jump at school and then sprinted into action. As her toes reached the edge of the pit she launched herself into the air and grabbed the pipe. Her fingers gripped the pipe firmly and the support brackets groaned but did not give way. Muscles burning, she began to work her way hand over hand along the pipe. To her surprise her hands did not ache as much as she had expected. Her enhanced strength was working even better than she had imagined. Slowly but surely she continued to make her way along the pipe. Every so often she looked down into the black pit below, wondering why the ceiling lights seemed unable to illuminate what was at the bottom.

Although she was now most of the way across, she began to sense that she was being watched. Looking behind her she could not see anyone following her; nor was there anyone ahead waiting for her. It was then that she felt something brush against her foot. Looking down again she saw a slimy black tentacle reaching up out of the gloom to get her. Horrified, she lashed out with her other foot, and knocked the tentacle away and continued to climb along the pipe faster than ever. What kind of monsters did the princess have in the Hollow Earth? Concentrating on her hand holds, she was almost at the end of the pipe when she felt something touching both her feet. Looking down again she saw dozens of writhing black tentacles reaching up for her. Some were thin tendrils, like slimy dark string. Others were like those of an octopus, black with suckers and writhing frantically. Muscles suddenly aching, she lifted her legs up out of reach and hung there for a moment. To her horror, the bigger tentacles were reaching up in front of her to block her escape. Then she saw that other tentacles were sliding their way up the walls on each side of her, while blobs of the living slime began to appear on the ceiling above her. It was as if the black substance was oozing out of the tiny cracks. These quickly began to merge together and surround where her hands gripped the pipe. Then from the darkness below a black blob spat up at her and hit her leg. To her horror she could feel it moving as if it was trying to eat through her pressure suit. Instinctively she kicked it off and knew she only had one chance to escape. Making one final effort she unhooked her feet and swung herself back as far as she could and then threw herself forward; letting go of the pipe at the last moment. The tentacles below lashed out at her as she passed over them and landed heavily on her back on the tunnel floor. Groaning loudly she looked back and saw that she was no longer being chased by them and realised that she was safely out of reach of the tentacles.

*

The narrow passage Lucy was travelling down suddenly opened up into a small, square room. All the walls and floor were brilliant white and seamless. Immediately her heightened intelligence caused her to pause for a moment. Why did the passage change? She could see that on the other side of the white room the passage continued as normal. She guessed the tunnel was part of the access way used to carry out maintenance.

Cautiously she stepped into it.

The room was a white walled box about twenty feet long. As she took another step forward lots of inch thick tubes extended from the walls, blocking the way. They looked solid and part of some complex machine. She reached out and touched one with her hands. It felt like cold metal. Suddenly dozens of others silently slid out of the wall behind her, blocking her escape. She was imprisoned. Fighting her rising panic, she crouched down and looked along the tunnel in the direction she wanted to go. Despite the many poles, she saw that if she squeezed and twisted her body through the correct gaps she could get through to the other side. However as she went to move between the first few, more poles extended behind her, this time from the ceiling and floor. Now she was truly trapped like someone behind prison bars. She had no choice except to go forward.

First she got down onto her belly and crawled under several layers of horizontal poles and then got to her knees ready to step over through the next gap. Immediately, more poles slid out of the ceiling and floor, narrowing her only way forward even more. It was then she realised that she was trapped in a mathematical security puzzle. Even worse, she realised that some of the new poles were changing temperature. One second they were ice cold to the touch, the next second they were too hot to hold. There was only one way through and she had no choice but to twist and contort her body through the maze of poles.

Chapter Seventeen

The passage that Bridgid was travelling down came to an abrupt end and opened out onto yet another large underground cavern. This one was different. The high ceiling was covered in green fungus which gave off a dim glow. The cavern seemed to be a place where lots of large tunnels and shafts converged. But there was no sign of anything which looked like the main base and she began to worry that she had been travelling in the wrong direction.

However in the centre of the cavern she saw dozens of giant domed greenhouses filled with strange looking vegetation. Some looked like huge fungus with brightly coloured caps. Others looked like giant pea pods which hung from metal frames. Bridged also noticed that ant-like insects, the size of cats were swarming in all the domes, busy harvesting the fully grown foliage and putting the sliced pieces into processing machinery. These looked like garden shredding machines. The mashed material was then being squirted along pipes to food production areas elsewhere in the cavern. Bridgid concluded that the insects were worker-slaves, under the control of Sekmet's computers. She also noted that entire root systems were growing down from the cavern roof. The roots moved like they had minds of their own; seeking out victims to snatch. She guessed that Sekmet was re-starting these food production facilities for the Giants and Titans. Not knowing where to go next she took out her tracker and tried to get a fresh indication of what direction to take.

Suddenly two combat drones dropped from concealed tubes in the ceiling and flew at her, one from each side. These were different from the type she had encountered before, as they had two additional mechanical arms as well as the six pipe weapons. They swooped at her so fast that she had no time to react. With frightening speed their telescopic arms grabbed her wrists and ankles and then lifted her upside down and high into the air.

*

George continued to grow more excited as he successfully brought to life the second Cyclops. Under the guidance of Hades he had learned how to make them move in unison or make completely independent actions. Now they stood to attention like soldiers in front of him on the other side of the observation window.

Hades rubbed his hands together with joy. "Excellent! Excellent! This is working better than I could have ever imagined. Now we need to see if you can control something bigger."

Pointing at a larger tube which was hanging from the ceiling, he used his wrist control to guide the grab to position the tube over the grill in the floor. The bottom of the tube opened and a strange shape slid out, surrounded by green and blue slime. The organic goo slowly drained away through the grill leaving a misshapen figure slumped on the floor. They could see it was still covered in smears of pus and trails of purple slime.

Straight away without waiting for orders from Hades, George focused his mind on the shape and it began to rise to its feet. Immediately he realised that this was different from the Cyclops. It was not just several times bigger but was an entirely different shape. The creature, for that was what it was; stood on all fours like a lizard and had a long tail which it curled out from under its belly and flicked into the air. Next its strangely shaped slime covered head extended from out of the front of the body, like a tortoise head emerging from its shell. To George's amazement the head suddenly separated into nine writhing serpents, each moving independently. He gasped. It had nine snake heads. It was a Hydra!

Hades patted the boy on the back. "Well done. Don't worry. It's only a baby Hydra. A fully grown one is over fifty feet long and has scales thicker than tank armour."

George nodded in admiration; he could already feel that his mind had complete control over it. Although it had lots of heads with a brain in each, he was able to manipulate the creature to do what he wanted. Even before Hades could order him, he had already got it to pace around the chamber and stretch all its muscles.

Hades grinned at the eagerness with which George was enjoying himself. "Now boy, we need to test your powers even more. First bring to life another Cyclops and get all three under your control. Then attack the Hydra with them. See if you can also manipulate the Hydra to use its multiple heads to defend itself."

George hesitated for a moment, thinking that controlling two opposing forces in a pitch battle would be impossible. Then he grinned widely at the thought of this challenge, and began to concentrate. If he could do this, then he could control all the Giants and Titans. He would be unstoppable!

Stood behind him was Prince Cronus, delighted that the surface boy was not just totally under their control, but now a willing participant.

*

Anne's fingers and knuckles were white with the strain of holding onto the pipe, and she flexed her hands to get the colour back into them. She gritted her teeth and lay still on the floor for a moment, breathing heavily, slowly relaxing her hands and arms until the pain subsided. She was glad she had enhanced strength otherwise she would never have made it across the monster pit. Looking back over her left shoulder, she sighed with relief when she saw that none of the black slime was following her.

Sitting up she took out her tracker to confirm that she was still heading in the right direction, then she stood up and strode down the passage at a brisk pace.

*

Lucy's enhanced mathematical mind allowed her to clearly see a way through the crisscross of poles. Every time she squeezed through the next set of barriers more poles slid out in front of her to restrict her way. And if she tried to go back to find a different route, some poles became ice cold or burning hot. In response she paused each time and used her newfound power to spy a new way through. This time she used the poles in front of her like a climbing frame and scrambled to the top and edged between the ceiling and the highest horizontal pole. Climbing over the poles she wriggled her way down between them until she was in the middle. To anyone else it would look as if she was completely caged; but with one final wriggle she squeezed through the last set of poles and flopped onto the floor exhausted.

After taking a deep breath she sat up and checked her tracker to make certain that she was still on course.

Pleased with herself she stood up and continued to walk down the passage.

*

Bridgid was suspended helplessly in the air by the two drones. No matter how hard she squirmed she could not get free or reach any of her weapons. She had been suspended like this for what seemed ages, but what she could not understand was why they had not killed her.

As if in answer to her thoughts a loud voice shouted sarcastically from behind and the princess flew into view on a hover-board. "My combat drones automatically informed me that they had caught an intruder!"

The board had emerged from a tunnel in the left side of the chamber and the princess stopped it so she could hover with her face level with Bridgid's upside down face. Then she leaned forward against the board's safety rail so her face was close to Bridgid's.

"So you survived the destruction of your craft. Are there any other survivors?"

"Just me," lied Bridgid.

The princess chuckled in disbelief. "I don't believe you. So I'll send more drones to search the tunnels. I'll also summon my craft to come and collect us and then join the search myself."

She put her face even closer to Bridgid's and gave a sly grin. "If there are any other survivors they will soon be captured. Then you will tell me everything I want to know, such as where you have come from and why you are here."

The deputy commander said nothing, but felt a chill run down her spine.

*

Anne continued down the sloping passage as fast as she could. Feeling remarkably refreshed after the ordeal she started to jog at a fast but steady pace. Time was passing and she feared what might be happening to George. The sooner she got to the main base the better.

The further she went down the passage, the more she became aware of a humming noise. The nearer she got to its source the more she also became aware of a vibration in the walls and floor. Whatever it was she guessed that it was powerful machinery somewhere near her passage.

As the lighting in the passage became fainter she grew more cautious. A few yards later she came to a sharp turn to the right and found her way blocked by a series of large spinning ventilation fans. The passage went into a wide, circular metal tube several times her height. The tube was about twenty feet long and had four fans spaced out in it, one behind the other. The metal blades of the fans were long and thin, filling the full width of the tube. The closer she got to them, the more she was aware of the air being pulled towards them through what she guessed was a giant air purification and distribution system.

Stopping at a safe distance she watched the spinning blades for a few minutes and noticed that they were rotating at different speeds. She also noted that the space between each of the four fans was wide enough for a person to stand safely in. Making a loud sigh she realised that her enhanced speed might allow her to get past the first fan and then pause to wait for the next to rotate into a position for her to get through. If she got the sequence correct and she was fast enough she would get past all four. Or so she hoped.

*

Lucy found that the long sloping passage she was following divided into two. Taking out the tracker it clearly indicated that she should go to the left. The passage was narrower and darker than the previous one and she was wary of falling prey of another obstacle.

Despite this she started down the passage at a steady pace, wishing that she had a hand torch to see what was ahead. But no matter how scared she felt, she pressed on for the sake of George.

Then she froze. There was the sound of movement behind her. She turned and looked but could not see anything. All she could see was the rectangle of light from the wider passage she had left behind.

And then a shiver of fear shot up her spine. A silhouetted figure moved into view and blocked the rectangle of light. It was a combat drone! Lucy immediately turned and fled down the passage as fast as she could, pursued by the drone. She felt her heart pounding in her chest and she gasped and wheezed loudly as she struggled to keep ahead of the flying killing machine. She knew she was not fit enough to out run it. If only she had her sisters enhanced powers! Trapped in the confines of this passage she had no way of fighting off the drone. And then her luck changed, as ahead of her she saw the end of the passage and bright blue light beyond it.

Spurred on by the chance of escape she sprinted the last few yards and jumped out of the passage and into the cavern beyond. Before she hit the ground her ankles were grabbed from above and she was pulled into the air. To her horror she realised that a second drone had been waiting for her. The one in the passage had deliberately chased her into its clutches! These drones were slightly different from the ones she had seen before and had two telescopic arms with metal claws. Crying out in horror, her voice echoed loudly around the chamber.

Chapter Eighteen

Anne timed her first jump correctly and passed between the spinning blades of the first fan with ease; landing nimbly on both feet and coming to a dead stop. If she had stumbled forward beyond the safety of the gap she would have gone head first into the rotating blades of the second fan and been chopped into pieces. Safe, she wiped the sweat from her brow and took a few deep breaths to force her to concentrate. Having prepared herself she made a mad leap through the next set of blades. She landed on her tip toes again and wobbled for a moment but managed to stop herself from toppling forward into the next set of blades.

Swallowing hard she silently thanked her enhanced abilities and watched the rotation speed of the third fan. She noticed that the third and fourth fans were rotating at almost the same speed and decided to get through both sets at the same time. It was a risk, but she needed to find George as fast as possible and could not afford any more delays. Lowering herself into a semi-sprinting position she sprang head first through the third fan and landed on her hands; then immediately cart wheeled feet first past the last fan. As she landed safely on both feet she felt a lock of her hair cut by the fourth fans blades. Looking back she saw several strands of the blue hair lying on the floor. She mused that the last jump really had been a close shave!

*

Lucy hung in midair under the drone, suspended by her ankles. She felt panic filling her, smothering any rational thought. Next the drone which had been chasing her emerged from the passage and flew up to hover level with her. Slowly its metallic tentacles rose towards her face menacingly, forcing Lucy to turn away in horror. Cringing, she waited for the killer blow to hit her, but to her surprise nothing happened. Minutes passed and eventually she half opened one eye and looked around her. Why was she still alive?

Realising that the drone was just hovering and watching over her, she fully opened both eyes and looked around the large cavern she was in. Her enhanced mind was curious to see where she was. Even from her upside down position she could see that it had a large lake in the middle with dozens of big water pipes coming out of it. The metal pipes pumped the water into a large metal tank set in the ceiling where it was purified and then pumped around the underground base. She also noticed the entrances to several large tunnels on the far side of the lake. This she guessed was the River Styx of Greek mythology, which formed the boundary between the Earth and the underworld of Hades.

The lake was fed by a large spring which bubbled up at its centre, causing small waves to ripple across its surface at regular intervals. But to Lucy's amazement the lake fed into a river which went up a series of waterfalls. The water was going uphill! Lucy blinked and looked again, but her eyes were not deceiving her, the water was defying gravity. It must be part a river system which made its way to the surface.

Lucy also noticed that there were large fish swimming in the crystal clear water. They were a type of fish she had never seen before; as they had two heads and rows of red swivelling eyes along their bodies. Several of them started to swim under where she was suspended. She hoped that they were not meat eaters.

Suddenly her face turned into a vision of horror as she saw the princess's spacecraft fly out of one of the large tunnels opposite and come straight over to where she was held captive.

In response to its arrival, the drone holding Lucy rose higher into the air to allow the craft to stop and hover directly underneath them. Then a circular air lock opened in the top of the craft and the drone dropped her inside.

*

Anne sprinted down the passage as fast as she could. Her tracker had showed that she was still on course to find George and she was more anxious than ever to get to the base. She also wondered what had happened to Lucy and Bridgid. Would she meet them at the base?

As she approached the end of the passage she noticed that the light was changing. The light ahead glowed bright red and she realised why as she emerged into a huge cavern. In the centre of the vast expanse was a lava lake. The red and white liquid spat and bubbled like hot fat in a frying pan. Anne immediately felt the heat on her face even though she was several hundred feet away from the edge of the lava. The lake looked as if it was artificial because its edge was perfectly circular and had large black pipes pumping the hot liquid out and into tunnels. Other pieces of equipment were built into the shore around the lake and she guessed they were part of some elaborate heat distribution system. They were heavy-looking machines designed to withstand the extreme heat of the lava, but they all looked automated. No sign of any people or robots.

In the centre of the lava lake there was a volcano-shaped island; out of which oozed fresh molten magma. Around the island was a wall and a circle of lava fountains, which acted as filters, only allowing the purest liquid to flow into the lake. Even with her enhanced strength and this distance away from the lava, she felt the heat beginning to tingle on her skin. Stepping back towards the cavern wall she consulted the tracker again to see which of the other tunnels to head for. She also noted that some of the tunnels opposite were large enough to take huge vehicles.

It was then Anne became aware of something behind her. Without waiting for it to get close she somersaulted backwards high into the air and landed perfectly on both feet. For a moment she was confident; each time she used her enhanced strength, she was getting better. Then to her horror she saw that a flying drone had been sneaking up on her.

Confused by her unexpected escape, the drone hovered unmoving for a moment, but then located her and rotated to face her. Anne's terror was increased when she saw that this drone had telescopic arms as well as its weapons tubes. Suddenly it lunged at her, its tentacle-arms snapping and slashing!

*

Lucy awoke to find herself sitting in a metal chair in the control bridge of the princess's craft. Still in a state of shock and surprise she tried to move but found that her wrists and ankles were fixed to the legs and arms of the chair with metal straps. She was also horrified to find that her gasp of fear was stifled by a wide piece of metallic tape was over her mouth.

Fighting back the panic, she looked to her left and saw that Bridgid was also strapped to a chair in the same way. She was also struggling against her bonds, but could not get free either. The only other person in the room was the princess, who stood in the middle of the wide glass viewing screen at the front of the craft. She stood with her back to them, her hands clasped together in the small of her back. To Lucy she looked supremely confident. Without bothering to turn to face them, Sekmet began talking in a strong, commanding voice.

"Do not even bother to try and get free. You are my prisoners now and the other human brat has just been caught. This craft will only take a few minutes to fly through the connecting tunnel to get to the heat generation cavern where she is being held."

In response Bridgid struggled against her bonds again, but could not break free. Hearing her prisoners' struggles, the princess turned to face them. "The human brat will soon be my prisoner as well. Then when I get you all back to my Command Centre you will tell me everything I want to know!"

Fearing the worst, Lucy and Bridgid frantically struggled again, even though in their hearts they knew it was hopeless.

*

Anne was battling the drone to a standstill. Using her enhanced strength and agility, she was jumping, bouncing and somersaulting out of the drone's reach every time it grabbed for her.

Despite her success, she wondered why it had not opened fire on her. As fast as she was, there was no way she could dodge its laser beams or energy blasts. Yet it did not open fire. Between each frantic somersault she concluded that the drone had been sent to catch her, not kill her. Sekmet must know where she is!

But she knew that she must avoid being caught at all costs; otherwise how would she be able to save George?

Even as her options raced through her mind, she saw the saucer shaped craft fly out of the large tunnel on the far side of the cavern and immediately stop to hover high over the lava lake. "Sekmet's craft!" hissed Anne nervously under her breath, as she completed another summersault.

She realised that she had to escape without Sekmet seeing her. She had to make the princess think that she had been killed in this battle with the combat drone. There was just one chance. And it was a very risky chance. A risk that could get her killed for real.

Anne sprinted away from the drone as fast as she could towards one of the pipes which carried the molten lava. The drone immediately flew after her. Her heart pounding in her mouth, Anne leapt at the pipe just as the drone caught up with her. Before it could grab her she somersaulted over the pipe, out of its reach. But the drone could not stop in time and crashed into the pipe at full speed. The drone exploded on impact, and a split second later the lava in the pipe spurted out and sent a wall of flame in all directions.

Anne landed on her feet, but was unexpectedly blown by the blast into the air again, out of sight of the princess's craft. As she span out of control Anne crashed into a metal grill set into the cavern wall. The rusty metal immediately gave way and she fell into a steep metal shaft. Before she realised what was happening, she was tumbling down it, out of control.

Chapter Nineteen

The explosion around Anne was clearly seen by everyone on Sekmet's craft.

Lucy was shattered. She had just seen her big sister blown to bits. If she was not gagged she would have screamed. Instead huge tears began to well in her eyes, roll down her cheeks and over the metallic tape.

Bridgid groaned with rage as well, and tried to free herself again, sweat pouring down her face with the effort.

The princess turned to face them, her face filled with anger. "No matter if the girl has been blown up. I can still get all the information I need from the two of you."

*

Anne tumbled backwards in free fall down the square metal shaft for several seconds, before she crashed into another rusty metal grill. The grill buckled and broke free from its surround and fell to the floor, with Anne on top. As she lay stunned, clouds of dust and bits of rusty metal fell down the shaft onto her, forming a fine layer. She deliberately lay still for a moment, making sure that she did not have any broken bones or internal pains. She was thankful for the grill absorbing some of the impact of the fall and her enhanced strength protecting her; knowing that they had saved her from certain death.

Regaining her composure, she carefully stood up and dusted herself off. Looking around she saw that she was in a large circular metal pipe, lit by occasional blue lights set into the top. Taking out the tracker she studied it for a moment, saw that the signals were stronger in one direction and began to walk that way.

*

George looked on approvingly. The three Cyclops that he had revived, now lay dead on the floor of the chamber, their green blood oozing through the grills. The baby Hydra stood triumphant in front of the observation window and was looking directly at George. Four of its serpent heads were missing; pulled off by the attacking Cyclops, but even as he watched four new ones began to grow to replace them.

From behind George, Prince Cronus laughed out loud with pleasure and Hades rubbed his hands together with glee. The surface boy was now on their side. The combination of hypnotism and the excitement of having such personal power had taken over the boy's normal personality!

Hades spoke to the boy, this time taking him into his confidence like a trusted friend.

"In this Hollow Earth ten thousand years ago I secretly created many genetically engineered creatures. Creatures which I was growing for King Zektor to use to destroy the Crystal Lords of Atlantis so he could take control of all the Zodiac Crystals for himself. Before I had fully developed them, Atlantis was destroyed and I had no choice but to put all my creations into suspended animation."

He pointed his finger at a flat wall on the opposite side of the Central Administration Laboratory and it became a large screen, showing a scene from elsewhere in the underground complex. As the picture panned around the cavern, it showed a series of large transparent tubes containing liquid and a wide variety of bodies. All were unmoving, but George knew that they were in a deep sleep.

Hades walked over and stood shoulder to shoulder with George, eager to show off his handiwork.

"All of my creations have become myths and legends among the human beings. Vulcan the Roman fire God. Prometheus the Greek God who stole fire. Neptune the Roman name for the Greek God Poseidon. The Phoenix who can resurrect itself from flames. Griffin, part eagle, part lion. Basilisk, with its wings, crest and claws of a cock and reptilian body. Hydra, the Greek nine headed serpent monster. I am particularly pleased with how that creation turned out. The full size one is utterly ferocious. If one head is cut off another grows in its place!

"Another favourite of mine, is the Gorgon. In Greek mythology; she is a monster with writhing, venomous snakes for hair. The Chimera, composite goat-lion-serpent monster belching forth fire, again from Greek legend. The Sphinx of ancient Egypt, the human headed lion. These were to be bred in large numbers as guards, to support my Cyclops shock troops. The Minotaur was also bred as troops for an army; part bull, part man; again from legend. Then I bred a Centaur, a horse with a human body and head. Then I wanted an army of flying monsters so I created the Harpy, a woman headed bird with a vulture's body and claws.

"And finally, you have already met my personal favourite; the Cyclops. The brutish giant of Greek mythology. A powerful man with a single eye in the middle of its head. This is what I chose to be the first of my creations to put into mass production."

George's eyes opened impossibly wide; he was anxious to move on to the next test. He wanted to bring some of the huge monsters to life and take control of them.

*

Sekmet's craft entered the landing area through another opened metal iris, and stopped to hover over a large circular platform. The platform was attached to a tubular walkway which led into a domed building, which jutted out the rock face of the huge cavern. There was an identical platform and walkway on the other side of the building. It was empty, as Prince Cronus's craft had been destroyed on the Earth's surface.

Sekmet's craft descended silently and landed on its designated platform. After a few minutes the door opened in the underside of the craft and the hover-board slowly flew out. Stood confidently on the front was the princess, while behind her knelt Bridgid and Lucy, hands tied behind their backs. They both wore metal collars similar to dogs which had chains fastened to the deck of the hover-board in front of them, forcing their bodies forward into a submissive crouching position.

Lucy felt dreadful. Anne was dead, George was under their control and she and Bridgid were helpless prisoners. Trying to take her mind off her despair, she turned her head sideways to see where they were. She immediately saw that under the complex landing area was a lake of bubbling lava. The landing area extended from the side of the cavern wall and she guessed that a force field prevented the lava lake below from rising to engulf it.

Her enhanced mind began to race even though her situation was desperate. She calculated that if the base's main power source was shut down, then the lava would erupt and destroy it. If only she could get free she could do it!

Seconds later the hover-board entered the main reception area and the door slid shut behind them with a loud clang.

*

Anne progressed down the pipe as fast as she could. At intervals there were smaller pipes which branched off, or openings covered with metal grills. Some of the openings were the size of her hand while others were big enough to crawl through, if they weren't barred. Ever since she had entered the pipe she had been aware that she was alone, more alone than ever before. Except for the echoes of her foot steps as she clanked along the pipe, there was no sound. Perhaps more than ever she was suddenly aware that she was trapped miles underground, with millions of tonnes of rock above her head.

Fighting back the claustrophobic fears, she pressed on down the gently sloping pipe, her echoes clanking ahead of her.

After a while she came to an intersection and took the larger pipe which went to the right. A short while later she became aware of the sound of pumps and machinery. Moving forward cautiously she came to another of the grill-covered openings on her left. Stopping to sneak a look inside she saw a large rock-ceilinged chamber, lined with rows of massive glass tubes. Other tubes were the size of normal people. All, however, were linked together by rows of pipes which carried various coloured liquid. Every tube also had control panels on the sides. Set into the cavern roof were a series of gantries and overhead crane systems. Looking carefully she saw that each tube was filled with green liquid and suspended in it were hideous looking creatures. Luckily they all looked to be either asleep or dead. However Anne visibly winced as she studied each one in detail. Some tubes had creatures with several heads; others were winged monsters with claws and malformed bodies. To her horror, others looked as if humans and animals had been joined together. She could not get over how different the sizes of the tubes were or the types of creatures inside them. Some were the size of normal humans while others were as big as a house!

She did not know what this place was and nor did she want to. She guessed that these were the Giants and Titans of legend; the results of monstrous experiments carried out in the mythical Tartarus. A shiver of fear ran down her spine and she quietly stepped away from the grill and continued to creep down the pipe in the direction she had been going.

*

Prince Cronus watched George from behind at a safe distance where he could not be overheard. Next to Cronus stood Hades, eager to discuss matters with the prince.

"The boy is remarkable. His ability to revive all my creations is guaranteed. I just need to perform a few more tests and then we can begin to revive all the Giants and Titans in sequence."

Cronus nodded. "Just make sure that you do not let slip to the boy that we have captured one of his sisters and that the other is presumed dead. I do not want him losing his focus. He must remain tricked into helping us revive your creations!"

Hades nodded in silent agreement and looked back at George. Even as the squat little man studied the boy from behind, he could see him continuing to experiment with his control over the infant Hydra. The boy was the answer to their prayers. He would provide them with an army to conquer the surface world and wipe out the human race!

Chapter Twenty

The interrogation room in which the princess had imprisoned Bridgid and Lucy was square, all metal with a high ceiling. The only source of illumination was a series of red lights set into recesses high in the walls. Their eerie glow cast strange shadows throughout the room.

The princess stood by a circular control table set in the middle of the room. On its flat top was spread an array of medical type instruments and inset into it were control buttons and computer screens.

Lucy was imprisoned on one side of the room, while Bridgid was held on the other. Bridgid was now only clad in a silver metallic leotard and was strapped into a circular frame spread-eagled and helpless. Each wrist and ankle was held in place to the frame by wide metal cuffs. The silver tape was still over her mouth. All the while she was constantly pulling and twisting against the cuffs so hard that perspiration ran down her face, but there was no way to get free. The circular frame was floating free from the wall, held in place by magnets positioned around the room. The princess was able to control the angle of the frame, move it around the room and rotate it upside down, to increase the captive's discomfort. For amusement she had set the frame to spin slowly upside down, to disorientate Bridgid, while she turned her attention to Lucy.

Lucy was captive on the other side of the room and like Bridgid was only dressed in a silver leotard. Sekmet had used a molecule disruptor ray to dissolve their high pressure flight suits in order to attach heart monitoring sensor pads onto their arms and legs. Lucy was suspended from the ceiling by a chain made of glittering crystals. Her arms were tied together above her head and attached to a ring at the end of the crystal chain. She had been hoisted up so that her toes could only just touch the floor. Her ankles were tied together with a crystal chain. She too was still gagged. The whole time that she had been in the room she had constantly kept her gaze on Sekmet, fearful of what she was planning to do to them. To make things worse, her body's special enhancements were starting to wear off and her green skin was beginning to pale. Even as she looked down at her legs, her skin was returning to its normal pale pink.

Lucy and Bridgid's other belongings had been piled up on the table, next to the bag containing Bridgid's bombs.

At length the princess finished what she was doing on the table and turned to face Lucy.

"You are probably wondering why I have not removed your gags, if I am going to force you to tell me your secrets. But it is not necessary, as my instruments can read your thoughts. However, experiencing my mind probe can be a painful experience. The more you resist, the worse it is. But in the end there is no way to fight my mind probe device. Bridgid is clearly strong and will resist for the longest. You, however, are a weak human and will offer little resistance, especially as your Atlantis enhancements are beginning to wear off. I can clearly see that you are no longer dark green."

The princess gave Lucy a long sinister stare, the red glow of the room's lights casting strange shadows across her face. "The device I am going to use on you also acts as a body scanner. So as it reads your mind for relevant information, it will also give me your complete biological profile, both your human part and the traces of Atlantis enhancements which are still in you!"

Without further explanation, she picked off the table a device that looked like a silver cycling helmet and placed it on Lucy's head. The girl tried to resist, mumbling groans of protest and twisting her head from side to side, but with effort the princess forced it on and strapped it tightly into place, buckling it under her chin. The helmet had multiple glowing wires woven into it and rows of tiny pulsating lights. Out of the front of the helmet Sekmet extended four narrow tubes. These she inserted up Lucy's nose and into her ears. This caused the prisoner to resist again as they went deep inside. Next the princess pressed some controls on the side of the helmet and it began to hum and glow. Lucy began to shake wildly and then as suddenly as she started, she stopped shaking.

Finally her eyes opened uncontrollably, as if she could see something terrifying and then they rolled upwards and back into her head.

*

Anne continued along the pipe as fast as she could without attracting attention. Now that she had seen some of Hades' monstrous creations she knew more than ever that she had to rescue George before he could be used to revive them.

And what of Lucy and Bridgid?

Suddenly she froze as she heard a strange howl echo along the pipe towards her. Yet instead of obeying the urge to run away, Anne used her enhanced abilities to gain courage to press on. Speeding up her pace, she rounded a corner and found yet another grill set into the side of the pipe. Just as she was about to peer through it another howl assaulted her ears and she realised it was coming from the other side. Plucking up even more courage she leant forward and peered through. On the other side of the grill she saw a large chamber filled with more tubes. However these were all normal size and contained humanoid shapes. Her eyes widened with interest as she saw that several tubes had opened and standing close by were two Cyclops.

They were standing to attention, like living statues, but looking close she could see their chests rising and falling. As each one was being brought back to life, it was letting out a howl of delight. Instinctively she knew that this was George's handiwork. He was already using his Atlantis DNA to bring the monsters to life!

Stepping back from the grill she turned and continued down the pipe as fast as she could.

*

The princess removed the mind probe from Lucy and placed it back on the table, a satisfied grin on her face.

"Now that did not take too long did it Lucy? I said that you would be unable to resist my mind probe."

Lucy swayed exhausted from the crystal chain, relieved that the ordeal was over. Her body had now fully returned to normal leaving no trace of its green appearance. Meanwhile the princess studied the instrument data on the control table.

"What this information tells me is that your DNA has the same Atlantis gene as your brother George. That is great news for us. Hades will be able to use you to revive more Giants and Titans! By combining your abilities, you and your brother will be able to control an entire army of our monsters and guarantee our re-conquest of the surface world.

Regarding the temporary change of your skin colour, my data also tells me that our rivals used the technology on their craft to save you. This resulted in a temporary change to your body. Most of its enhancements have already faded and the remainder will soon wear off."

Lucy became enraged at the thought of being used by Hades to revive the monsters in the Hollow Earth and made a vain attempt to get free; but failed.

Satisfied about the results she had got, the princess turned her attention to Bridgid. "Now it's your turn. I recognise you as one of my own race but I need to know who you are, where you came from and why you tried to stop us. Once I know where you have come from, we can plan to conquer your people as well the humans!"

Lifting the mind probe off the table she purposefully strode over to the deputy commander and stopped in front of her. "I know that you will try and resist me, but rest assured you will tell me everything I want to know!"

Chapter Twenty-One

Anne progressed along the pipe as best she could under the circumstances, her combination of fear, haste and determination forcing her heart to pump extremely fast. So much so, that the pounding in her chest seemed to be forcing its way into her throat. Only her focused determination kept her from panicking.

Her concentration was shattered by a howl from just up ahead. Easing forward cautiously she reached another grill and held her breath. Was this another chamber filled with Cyclops? Carefully she looked around the edge and peered in.

Sphinx!

There were row upon row of human sized sphinx! They were all standing to attention like an army frozen in time. Each one was about six feet tall and built like a top athlete. The only thing which made them different from normal was their lion-like heads. Anne immediately realised that they were the opposite of the giant statue in Egypt, which had a lion's body and a man's head. Looking closely, she realised that like the army of Cyclops, these had recently been released from their suspended animation tubes. The green slime they had been living in was still sliding off them and draining through grills in the chamber floor. They too were howling with delight at being revived.

Easing herself back into the pipe she breathed out deeply but quietly. She realised that George was starting to activate more and more of Hades' monsters. She now began to think the unthinkable. Was it too late to rescue her brother? By the time she found him would the only choice left be to stop George? And if so how would she stop her brother?

Avoiding any further thoughts on the dilemma, she continued along the pipe.

*

Hades patted George on the back as he returned to stand next to him.

"Well done boy, you now have full control of a nine-headed infant Hydra. Even as we speak I am starting the activation sequences of the first ranks of Cyclops and Sphinx warriors. Once they are all out of their incubation tubes you can begin to test your powers over multiple quantities of my creations."

George was now completely engrossed in his newfound power. He could not wait to extend his abilities. Now he voiced his thoughts for the first time.

"While we are waiting for all those to be released from their tubes, I want to test my powers on another infant monster."

Behind him, Cronus's eyes opened wide with surprise; the surface boy was now totally absorbed!

"Try a Griffin," he suggested. "We need to know if you are able to control something which can fly. That is even more complicated than a nine-headed Hydra."

"A Griffin?" questioned George without turning around.

Hades nodded enthusiastically "A splendid suggestion. A Griffin is a half lion half eagle creation I am very proud of. There is an infant one in the chamber with the Hydra. I will move the suspended animation tube into position and release it. Then George, my boy, we will see if you can control something which flies!"

*

The princess forced the mind probe onto the deputy commander's head, strapping it securely into place despite her resistance. Bridgid gave a muffled groan from behind the gag, but there was nothing she could do.

"The mind probe will take longer with you than it did with the human girl. But you cannot resist it forever." said Sekmet coldly as she held the victim's head firmly with both hands and stared directly into her eyes. Then she abruptly let go and stood back, watching with fascination as the probe began to work.

Bridgid twisted furiously in her harness for a few minutes, fighting as long as she could, but eventually her eyes lost focus, as if under hypnosis and then rolled back into her head. After a while the princess turned away and studied the data screens intently as the information began to appear. Her eyes slowly widened as she began to interpret the data and realise how much there was.

"You know far more than I imagined. You know what has happened to our race since Atlantis sank ten thousand years ago! You have the sequence of events all in order. First our father High King Zektor and his allies were in conflict with the twelve Crystal Lords of Atlantis about who should have control of the Atlantis crystals. The twelve Zodiac Crystals provided the power for the city and its defences but were accidently attracting uncontrollable energy spikes. These threatened to cause a catastrophic dimension shock over Atlantis.

"But both factions were thwarted when the crystals were seized by Jaxar and Davius and secretly hidden all over the world in different time periods. Davius had discovered a form of time travel and hid them so Atlantis would not be destroyed by the impending dimension shock. However Davius also wanted to make sure that neither the High King nor the Crystal Lords could have total control over them. That was why Davius and young Jaxar hid them across time, deliberately linked to specific historic events in the future, where no one would be able to get them and use their power.

"Shortly after they did this, Atlantis exploded because of the dimension shocks and everyone was killed. However, unknown to anyone except our father the High King, my brother and I were in this secret underground base. We were here with Hades, growing genetically engineered creatures to help him defeat the Crystal Lords.

"Thinking that the surface world had been destroyed and everyone killed, my brother and I put all the equipment down here into a sleep mode and incubated all our genetic creations, because our power sources would not last very long. Finally we put ourselves into suspended animation until our automated sensors detected a new source of power.

"But unknown to us, Jaxar and Davius had survived the explosion and escaped to the mainland British Isles and other survivors had got to Egypt. The survivors mixed with humans; that is how traces of Atlantis blood are in the DNA of some humans today."

Sekmat's eyes widened with excitement as she studied her instruments and continued to talk about the revelations she had discovered.

"But unknown to everyone, other people from Atlantis secretly escaped in a fleet of spacecraft before the explosion. They left the Earth in the craft to start a new life on a planet the other side of the galaxy. Since then they have built a thriving Atlantis-style civilisation on that planet!"

Stunned by what she had discovered, the princess stood back from the table and stroked her chin with her fingers, silent and deep in thought.

"This is a revelation, but it leaves even more questions unanswered. Firstly, what happened on the surface of the Earth that triggered our suspended animation chambers into reviving? Secondly, what made you send a spacecraft from your new planet to Earth and stop us reclaiming the surface world? How did you even know that we had woken up after ten thousand years?"

All the while the princess was talking, Bridgid began to revive and started to shake her head furiously in a fruitless attempt to dislodge the mind probe helmet. Chuckling sarcastically, Sekmet moved back to the controls and began to increase the probe's power.

"I need to probe you deeper to get those answers. You clearly have a mind block in place to prevent key information being extracted from you."

Immediately she passed her hand over a small panel on the table and Bridgid's eyes glazed over again and her body went ridged. On the other side of the room Lucy finally awoke and made faint groans of protest.

The princess ignored her and watched as the power in the probe increased. In response, the eerie red lights in the room flickered intermittently.

After several minutes Sekmet changed the settings on the controls and began to study the new readings. As she did, her eyes once again opened wide with surprise.

"So that's it! A present day young human boy, with the Atlantis blood in his DNA, re-discovered the secret of time travel and went on a quest to get all the crystals.

Despite the perils of going to twelve key historic events and having to fight to get each one, he succeeded and brought them all to the present time. The boy is English and is called James Lightwater. He succeeded in his secret mission to use them to prevent an alien invasion. But bringing them all back together after ten thousand years unleashed their combined power. After a tremendous struggle he succeeded in controlling their enormous energy. However after his victory he vanished. No one knows where he is, or even if he is still on Earth. However with such power at his disposal he has probably left the Earth, or gone travelling through time again."

The princess frowned and continued to study the data in more detail.

"But what this information also shows, is that unknown to James Lightwater, the power unleashed when the crystals were brought together activated our underground sensors and brought us out of suspended animation!"

She nodded and became even more excited as she scrutinised the data.

"At the same time your Atlantis-style civilisation on your new planet was also alerted to the combined power of the crystals. You also detected our equipment in the Hollow Earth coming out of their long sleep mode. So they sent you in your spacecraft to try and stop us from retaking the surface world and conquering the humans!"

Stepping forward she switched off the probe and gave a sly grin. Turning to Lucy she pointed menacingly at her with her right index finger, fixing her with her staring, all-white eyes. Next the princess's tiny pin-prick pupils fixed Lucy with an hypnotic trance.

"My mind probe has given me everything I could have dreamed of. Firstly, we will continue to use your brother George to reactivate our genetically engineered creatures. Secondly, we will use you just like him, to reactivate even more of our larger creatures! By using you both the combined army will guarantee that we can re-conquer the surface world."

Next she turned to face the deputy commander.

"Then we will force you to reveal the location of your home planet. Once we know that we will use our human slaves to build an invasion fleet and conquer your planet.

"Finally we will use our combined technologies to track down the boy James Lightwater and get the twelve Zodiac Crystals from him! They rightfully belong to my father and the heirs of ancient Atlantis! Once I have them, there will be nothing to stop me taking over the galaxy!"

She suddenly let out a booming laugh that echoed around the metal room, causing Lucy's blood to run cold. Now she truly understood the meaning of fear. She would be turned into a mindless slave of the Princess, just like her brother!

Bridgid also struggled against her bonds in vain, now realising that she would not be able to resist the mind probe. She would be forced to betray the exact location of her planet and what they knew about the whereabouts of the human boy who had the Zodiac Crystals!

Chapter Twenty-Two

George marvelled at the infant Griffin. It had the body of a normal sized lion but also had large eagle wings which extended from the ridge of its back. It also had a ferocious beaked head streaked with red feathers. It was amazing!

He had decided to mentally command the Hydra to stand motionless at the far side of the chamber while he concentrated on the Griffin. He was also aware that the chamber had a low ceiling and he would not be able to test the beast's flying ability. However he could test its hovering skills.

Watching from behind him stood Hades, astonished by the speed of the boy's progress. There was movement from behind and Prince Cronus came into the room and stood next to Hades.

"I have just had a message from Princess Sekmet. She has discovered an amazing amount of information from Bridgid and the surface girl Lucy. My sister has uncovered that the girl's abilities are the same as George's. As soon as she finishes with her interrogation of them, she will bring the surface girl here. Then we can hypnotise her into reviving some of the full size Titans and Giants!"

Hades grinned and rubbed his hands together; his body tingling with excitement.

"Within the hour we will have all my creations awake, under control and ready to attack the surface world!"

*

Anne crept along the metal pipe as quickly and quietly as possible, still using the tracker for guidance. Her heart was pounding in her chest as she realised that the closer she got to the centre of the base, the more danger there was of getting captured. But more worrying was that for several minutes now she had been feeling strange and a bit unsteady on her feet. Looking at her hands she saw that her skin was beginning to change colour. It was beginning to alternate between green and her normal pale pink. She was beginning to lose her powers!

Suddenly she stopped dead in her tracks as she heard a voice. Moving forward cautiously she arrived at a metal grill set in the side of the pipe. Filled with a mixture of fear and excitement, she peered inside. Looking down through the grill she saw Lucy, Bridgid and the princess. The grill covered an opening which was at the top of the interrogation room and was at least twenty feet above the floor. She could see that Lucy and Bridgid were held captive, but the princess was stood with her back to them, overlooking controls on a table. Alarmingly, Anne could feel her powers draining away; she would have to act quickly if she wanted to save her sister and Bridgid!

Putting the tracker away in a belt pouch she gripped the grill with both hands and pulled with all her might. She had to pull it open, get through the hole, jump down, and land on top of the princess without making any noise while she still had some of her enhanced strength left. Gritting her teeth she made one last extra effort and the grill came free in her hands. Even as she put it down on the floor of the pipe quietly, she saw that her hands were turning fully back to normal. Realising that she only had seconds left, she hurled herself through the manhole sized opening and fell into the room without time to aim herself.

Instead of landing on top of the princess she crashed onto the floor with a loud bang close by and lay stunned by the impact. Struggling to get up, she realised that all of her power had now gone. The princess stood speechless for a moment, astonished that Anne was alive and had broken into the base. Then she snapped out of her shock and pulled a small laser pistol from her belt.

"You are dead, human!"

*

Hades and Cronus stared in amazement at the way George had taken control of the Griffin. Having got it to flex and stretch itself fully awake, he now had it hovering in the chamber on fast-beating wings. The boy's eyes were wide with excitement as he stared at it through the glass viewing screen. To Hades amazement he could see the Griffin staring back at George, as if it was transfixed by the boy's hypnotic gaze.

Having completed all his tests, George commanded it to land and fold its wings back into position. Then he commanded the Hydra to walk over and stand next to it, like two strange warriors awaiting his orders.

Next the boy took a deep relaxing breath, then removed the wires which Hades had stuck to his head and let them drop to the floor. Next he stepped up to the door which connected to the chamber containing the two monsters. To Hades and Cronus's astonishment he pressed the access controls and the door slid aside and he stepped in and the door slid shut behind him. They both immediately rushed up to the observation window to peer inside and see what the boy was up to.

George was drunk with his power. He stepped up between the Hydra and Griffin and stroked them affectionately. They were his pets and he was their master.

*

Anne's head felt as if was still spinning as she struggled to her feet, all the while keeping her eyes on the princess and her pistol. She cursed that she had landed too far away to attack the woman, but there was nothing that she could do. There was no way to reach her before she fired. Instead she slowly backed two paces away and to the right. In response the princess stepped a few paces back and took aim at her, savouring the look of fear she could see on Anne's face.

Behind her Lucy hung in her chains, now fully awake. Immediately realising what was happening she crossed her chained ankles then swung her legs back behind her and then forwards, kicking her feet up at the last moment. This allowed her feet to flick up over the princess's head and drop down in front of her face; the chained ankles pulling back into her exposed throat. The sudden shock and girl's full body weight pulling against the front of her neck and face trapped the princess and dragged her to her knees. Instinctively she put her hands up to her throat but accidently dropped the pistol on to the floor.

Realising that Lucy might not be able to restrain Sekmet for long, Anne sprang forward and seized the pistol. Now in control, Anne knelt down to be at the princess's level, and poked the end of the gun up her nose.

"How do I free my sister and Bridgid?"

Realising she had no choice the princess nodded. "There is a tube of spray on the top of the control table behind you. Spray it onto their restraints and they will quickly dissolve."

Anne frowned, not trusting the princess. "How can unbreakable chains and tape just dissolve?"

Sekmet sneered at how primitive human technology still was. "The spray is designed to break down the molecular structure of specific materials. The mixture in the tube is designed to dissolve that type of crystal and metals."

Still distrusting, Anne stood up and backed her way towards the main table, all the while making sure that she kept the pistol pointed at the princess. Seeing the tube on the table she seized it and held it up in her free hand, yet still keeping the princess in view. Studying it, she thought it looked like an elaborate hair spray with a strange nozzle

Assuming it would work, her first instinct was to free her sister but then she hesitated. Bridgid was far more experienced at dealing with this sort of crisis than either Lucy or herself, so she should free her first. Still keeping the princess in view, she backed towards Bridgid. Despite being strapped into a circular frame spread-eagled and helpless, the deputy commander wriggled and groaned vigorously at Anne to urge her on. Each wrist and ankle was held in place to the frame by wide metal cuffs. The silver tape was still over her mouth. The circular frame floated free from the wall, held in place by magnets positioned around the room. While hiding in the pipe above the room, Anne had watched how Sekmet was able to move the frame using a control panel on the table top. Putting the spray down she altered the controls and guided the metal frame to float down to the floor. Then she picked up the tube and sprayed Bridgid's hands, feet and mouth. For a few seconds nothing happened then the metal straps and tape turned to powder and fell away.

From the other side of the room Sekmet scoffed. "Told you our superior technology works. But now you are free, so what! Where can you go? What can you do? You are trapped miles underground in our lair. All your efforts are in vain!"

Looking back over to the other side of the room, Anne saw that Lucy was still suspended from the ceiling by a chain made of glittering crystals. Her arms were still tied together above her head and attached to a ring at the end of the crystal chain. Her ankles tied together with a crystal chain which was still pinning the princess to the floor. From behind the tape Lucy urged Anne to set her free next.

Anne handed the pistol to Bridgid so she could keep Sekmet covered and moved closer to spray her sister. First she sprayed her ankles and stood back to watch. Then as the chains turned to powder Lucy uncrossed her ankles and released the princess. Immediately Anne ordered Sekmet to shuffle to one side and kneel with her hands on the back of her head; still under cover of the pistol which Bridgid had pointed at her. Then she sprayed Lucy's wrists and the chains fell away so Lucy's feet dropped safely to the floor. Finally, Anne sprayed the mouth tape and it too turned into dust.

Immediately Anne threw her arms around her and they just hugged each other and sobbed with joy.

Bridgid broke their reunion with stern words. "Time for that later. We still have to find your brother and stop him from raising the Titans. Not to mention destroying this underground labyrinth and escaping alive!"

Still kneeling with her hands on her head, Sekmet mocked them. "It's too late, you idiots. George has already converted to our side and passed all the tests. He is about to re-animate all our creations!"

Anne's eyes blazed with fury as she strode over to the princess. "I don't care. We haven't come all this way to give up now. We've overcome every obstacle you have put in our way, and we will defeat you yet!"

Bridgid shook her head in frustration "We need to act fast if we are going to succeed."

Lucy glared at the princess, still rubbing her wrists where the chains had cut in. "We need to decide what we are going to do with her. She can't be allowed to stop us!"

All three nodded thoughtfully and for the first time the princess looked worried.

Chapter Twenty-Three

George had returned to the Command Centre and stood next to Hades and the prince, eager to start the next phase of the plan.

Hades held a portable body scanner in his hands, pointing it at the boy and slowly moving it up and down. "George is in perfect health and his mental abilities are at full peak. We are clear to proceed with the next stage of the plan."

Cronus nodded with excitement and turned to leave the Command Centre. "I will go to prepare. I need to be in the Titan's storage chamber to activate the moles!"

"Moles?" said George.

Cronus paused and turned to face the boy, happy to take him into his confidence. "Yes, that is how we will get the Titans and Giants to the surface. We have a fleet of giant burrowing machines. They will drill tunnels up through the rock and once they have reached the surface, we will unleash all of Hades creations and they will fly or climb up."

George was impressed, eager to see his powers used to send the army of monsters to the surface and wreak havoc.

Cronus turned and left the room without saying any more. They were now so close to achieving their dreams he did not want to waste another moment.

He moved at his swiftest walking pace until he reached a transparent door, which slid open with a swishing sound. On the other side was a moving walkway which activated the moment he stepped onto it.

As he was swept along at breath taking speed he contemplated how fortunate they were. Now they not only had the boy with his enhanced abilities, but his equally endowed sister. Nothing could stop them. And with the information Sekmet had got from Bridgid they would eventually have a new planet to rule as well as Earth. At that moment the walkway ended and he stepped off onto the floor. A few strides took him to a circular hole in the metal floor. Below was a transparent hover tube which would take him deep under the city to where the moles were stored on standby. Without hesitation he jumped feet first into the hole and was whisked down to his destination.

*

In the interrogation room, Sekmet had been strapped into the same floating frame that Bridgid had been restrained in. Her mouth had also been taped. On her head was fitted the mind probe.

Her belt and wrist weapons had been removed and Bridgid was using the mind probe on her. Lucy and Bridgid were also back in their proper high pressure flying suits, having used Sekmet's molecule disruptor ray to reform them on their bodies. Also familiar with such equipment as the mind probe, Bridgid began studying what information she had got from Sekmet's mind.

"She is trying to resist me but I have broken down her defences and can now download the schematics of this base as well as where George is located. Her mind is also informing me how to get to the chambers where the Titans are stored."

"What do we do now?" questioned Lucy, still rubbing her sore wrists.

Walking away and out of earshot from the prisoner, Bridgid whispered to the two girls. "We don't have much time. We must trick Sekmet into helping us. It's only a matter of time before someone comes here to find out why she has not reported in to the Command Centre. We have to use her as a diversion. When they find her we must make sure that she sends people in the wrong direction from where we are really going. That will give us time to make our plan work!"

"Where are we actually going and what is the plan?" whispered Anne.

Bridgid whispered back "I will take my pack of bombs and Sekmet's wrist force field generator then get into the Titan's chamber. First I will plant the bombs and then make my way to the landing area where Sekmet's spacecraft is. I will meet you there. Meanwhile you two must get to the Command Centre and use the pistol as a makeshift bomb to destroy the power module. Set its energy cell to overload and then escape. Next find George and then the three of you rendezvous with me at Sekmet's craft. I will then pilot the craft to the surface just in time for us all to escape the explosions."

Anne looked sceptical, it seemed like a desperate plan, but realised that they did not have any other choice. Lucy nodded in agreement and tucked the pistol into her belt.

Bridgid then moved back into the centre of the room, raising her voice slightly as if continuing the conversation, but now loud enough for Sekmet to just hear.

"So it's agreed. We abandon your brother, now that he is helping the enemy. So instead we immediately escape by using Sekmet's craft. Then I will pilot us to my home planet on the other side of the galaxy!"

The three of them walked through the room's exit and Bridgid cast a crafty glance back at the struggling Sekmet. "We will be long gone before anyone finds her!"

*

In the Command Centre Hades contemplated how he would best use George and his sister. He was worried that the sight of his captive sister being brainwashed would shock him out of the hypnotic control he was under, even though the boy was wearing the head band control. However Hades needed to get the girl's powers fully operational as soon as possible. He decided that when Sekmet arrived with Lucy, he would keep her in a separate area out of the boy's sight. That way neither of them would be distracted from their tasks of reviving all the creatures. It would take time to awaken all the Titans and keep them under strict control. He did not want any of the creatures to break free and rampage through the underground base. By then Prince Cronus would have activated all the moles and started them tunnelling towards the surface.

The giant machines may have lain dormant for ten thousand years but once they had started to cut their way through the miles of rock they would reach the surface in a few hours. By then George and Lucy would have brought back to life thousands of Hades' monstrous creations and commanded them to start climbing to the surface.

*

Bridgid crept through the massive chamber containing the Titan tubes. The whole area vibrated with the sound of machinery, so much so that she could feel the shocks coming up through her boots. The chamber was also hot and humid, as the temperature within the large tubes began to rise. Through the transparent sides of some tubes she could see some of the creatures beginning to move in the green life-preserving liquid. She could see eyes beginning to focus on her and follow her as she walked past. She hoped that none of them got free before she had planted her bombs. Through the maze of hanging tubes she could also see the rows of large hanger doors cut into the rock walls at floor level. One at a time each was swinging open to reveal a dark interior. Then lights inside each hanger glowed into life revealing giant mechanical diggers. Each one had a pointed end ringed with metal teeth and sides covered in long rows of caterpillar tracks and metal claws.

"Moles! So that's how they intend to get the Giants and Titans to the surface."

Behind her she heard movement and turned to see more Titans were beginning to stir inside their tubes.

This spurred her on to plant her bombs and get out of the chamber. Each explosive device was like a plaster, which she peeled off its backing paper and stuck onto the base of a tube. In the middle of each plaster-bomb was a tiny flat bulb that changed from green to flashing red as she stroked it. Each one she set to detonate in thirty minutes. Moving swiftly she went from tube to tube until she had placed the last one.

"How did you get here?" boomed an angry voice from behind her. Whirling around she was confronted by Prince Cronus who stood on the far side of the chamber.

"How did you get free and where is my sister?" he continued with an even louder bellow.

Before Bridgid could react the Prince activated an alarm button on his wrist control. "Alert. Intruder in Titan chamber! Also check the interrogation room and see what has happened to Princess Sekmet and her prisoners!"

Without waiting for a response he pointed his wrist weapon at her and took aim. Instinctively she raised her right arm and activated the personal force field device on her wrist. A split second later the blast from his wrist weapon struck the shimmering blue force field and bounced off. Unfortunately the force of the impact knocked Bridgid backwards off her feet to land flat on her back. Sprawling outstretched, her wrist device accidently hit the floor and switched itself off. She suddenly found herself defenceless.

Chapter Twenty-Four

Hades gasped as he got the alert message from Cronus. "George stop! What you are doing. There are intruders in the base!" Despite the unexpected alarm, he was anxious not to reveal to the boy that his sister may be one of the intruders. The master scientist knew that he had to handle the situation carefully until he understood what was going on. He did not want to do anything that might shock George out of his mind control. Telling him that his sister might have escaped from her interrogation cell would probably do it.

"George you take the infant Hydra and Griffin with you and start searching the base. I will go directly to where the princess is and find out what is going on!"

Without hesitation the boy nodded towards the two creatures and they silently followed him out of the Command Centre like obedient dogs.

As soon as he was alone, Hades looked at the wrist control on his left hand and checked that the life sign displays of the prince and princess were still registering. To his relief he saw that both of them were alive, so he set off towards the interrogation cell as fast as he could.

*

Anne and Lucy arrived at the intersection of several corridors opposite the Command Centre, just in time to see Hades leaving it. Behind him the doors slid shut with a loud clang.

Hiding around the corner they pressed themselves against the metal walls of the corridor, and held their breath as they hoped that he would go down a different corridor looking for the princess. At least that was how they had planned it. To their relief he did, and the strange little man strode quickly away in the direction they had hoped.

Once he had gone, Anne led the way over to the closed entrance to the Command Centre and stopped in front of the sliding doors. After a moment she kicked the doors with frustration as the electronic lock on the wall next to them refused to automatically open the doors for the girls.

"Use the princess's wrist control device," whispered Lucy who stood close behind Anne.

Her sister immediately waved her left wrist in front of the flickering lock and it changed colours and the door panels slid open to reveal the interior of the Command Centre.

Lucy pushed past Anne and entered first. "Quickly, before we are discovered. Who knows how long it will take Hades to discover our tricks!"

Anne followed her younger sister in and the doors slid shut behind them.

The Command Centre was a large spherical metal room with glittering walls. In the centre was a raised crystal pillar on which hovered a glowing ball. Lucy gasped as she realised that it was a perfect replica of what the surface of the Earth looked like ten thousand years ago. On it Lucy saw marked where Atlantis had been as well as all the hidden bases around the world. The flat floor of the Command Centre was made of alternate rings of metal and strong glass. Through these glass sections Anne could see that there was a lake of molten lava far below, held in place by layers of invisible force fields. In front of the crystal pillar there was a raised metallic dais on which there was a complex electronic frame, which held the power module.

"The module is unguarded!" exclaimed Lucy.

Anne responded by taking out the pistol and handing it over to her sister with both hands. "We need to get this in position and set it to explode!"

*

The blast from the prince's wrist weapon struck Bridgid's personal force field and bounced off in a hail of sparks. Thankfully the force field had automatically switched itself back on without Bridgid having to touch it. Despite the protection, Bridgid was anxious to get something solid between her and the prince, as she did not know how long Sekmet's force field wrist generator would last.

Before the prince could fire again, she sprang sideways in one fluid movement, somersaulting through the air and landing behind the nearest tube.

Furious at his rival's agility, the prince fired at a vertical metal support strut on her left and tried to get the ricochet blasts to bounce behind the tube and hit Bridgid. To his disgust the blasts kept striking the metal strut but bounced in the wrong direction.

Meanwhile Bridgid squatted safely behind the large tube, her heart pounding wildly, but her mind planning what to do next. Her thoughts abruptly changed as more blasts struck the support struts close to her and sparks spat all over the place. She instantly knew that she had no choice but to break cover and fall back to a safer position before planning her next move.

Determined to get her, the prince ran forward and changed the angle of his attack. He was obsessed with bouncing his energy blasts off the support struts to explode behind the tube where Bridgid was hiding, despite knowing he must avoid hitting a tube with his blasts. However the instant he fired he realised the mistake he had made. The shots bounced at the wrong angle again, but this time hit the base of the tube. Its transparent sides immediately shattered and green slime squirted in all directions. A moment later the bottom of the tube broke away and the creature inside fell out amidst a torrent of green and yellow liquid.

Bridgid sprang back from the slime as it spread across the floor and pressed her back against the tube behind her.

Cursing loudly, Cronus stopped firing and stood back to avoid the liquid; but his gaze was focused on the creature in the centre. To his amazement it was already starting to stand on its two legs. Like somebody waking from a deep sleep it slowly stretched its arms above its head and stood erect. The man-shaped creature was at least twenty feet tall, with hairless blotchy red skin. Its head was bald with larger than normal red eyes and a mouth which was more like a large dark hole. At the rear of the 'hole' a fiery glow began to form.

Cronus smiled with a mixture of relief and satisfaction. "It's Vulcan, the Roman God of fire!" he shouted at Bridgid. "He will burn you to a crisp!"

Pointing at her, the prince commanded the giant to attack the startled woman. He knew that there was no way her personal force field could withstand Vulcan's full-flame blast.

*

Hades burst into the interrogation room and saw Sekmet suspended and helpless. He immediately strode to the central table and operated the controls which lowered the frame she was trapped in to the floor. Fearful of her obvious rage, he freed her without saying a word and then sprayed her face to make the tape evaporate.

The furious woman stamped her feet with child-like rage. "All the prisoners have escaped. They were freed by the oldest girl. The one we thought had been killed!"

"Where have they gone Princess?"

"They are intent on escape. They are going to use my spacecraft to get to the surface, then return to Bridgid's home world. I am so angry at being captured by them! Hades come with me to the landing area, we may still be able to stop them!"

*

In front of the crystal pillar, Lucy saw the raised metallic dais with the power module in. Carefully she found and opened a panel at the base and saw a recess just wide enough to wedge the pistol into. Anne carefully placed the weapon into the recess and then pressed several of the buttons on its handle. This set a timer for its tiny power source to overload and explode, just as Bridgid had shown her. Carefully she set the timer for thirty minutes. Standing back she made way for Lucy to put the panel back over the recess.

"What are you two traitors up to?" shouted a voice from the other side of the Command Centre.

Looking up, Anne and Lucy saw George standing in the open doorway. Behind him stood the infant Hydra and Griffin, blocking the girls escape route.

"You two traitors will never leave here alive," said George with an unusually loud voice, and then signalled the Hydra and Griffin to attack the two girls.

Chapter Twenty-Five

The towering Vulcan stood menacingly between Cronus and Bridgid. With every passing second the creatures face became less and less human-looking as it contorted into an ever-widening mouth and burning eyes.

"Blast her you stupid creature!" shouted the prince impatiently at the top of his voice. "Do as I command you!"

But the creature swayed as if confused. It may have been revived by George's mind-control, but as the boy was now distracted the creature was not yet under anyone's control. Instead Vulcan kept turning its head, looking first at Bridgid, then Cronus and then back at Bridgid.

"I said kill the woman!" bellowed Cronus, working himself up into a frenzy.

Enraged by the prince's constant shouting, Vulcan turned and spat a torrent of fire at him. Cronus was immediately engulfed in a ball of fire and flailed about helplessly.

Bridgid was stunned by Vulcan's confusion and uncontrollable rage. Quickly regaining her composure Bridgid took the opportunity to hide behind one of the bigger tubes until she could escape. Her heart was pounding in her throat like a drum as she felt the heat of Vulcan's breath spreading through the chamber. Plucking up enough courage, she looked back in the direction of Vulcan and saw Cronus's discarded wrist weapon was lying on the floor. It had clearly been damaged by the heat blast and it was starting to short-circuit, causing sparks to spit in all directions. Even as she watched, one of the large sparks struck Vulcan in the face; going straight down its gaping mouth. Immediately the tall creature gripped its head like it was suddenly in great pain and roared out loud.

From her hiding place, Bridgid stared open-mouthed as she saw the creature's head explode, filling the chamber with noise and flame. Still shocked, she covered her ears with her hands until the noise of the explosion had subsided. Finally she stood up and surveyed what was left of Cronus and Vulcan. Not much except two piles of smouldering ash! Composing herself, she sprinted out of the chamber towards the landing area.

*

Sekmet and Hades ran into the landing area at full speed, their lungs heaving as they gasped for air.

"Where are they?" questioned the little man between breaths, expecting to confront the girls. He swept his weapon from side to side, looking for targets, but no one came out to confront him.

Sekmet came to a stop beside him and quickly looked in all directions. She had expected to find the three escapees trying to steal her craft. Instead the landing area was silent and her craft was standing untouched in its launch position. There was no sign of anyone.

"They have tricked us!" she screamed at the top of her voice. "They must be after George and the power module. We need to get back to the Command Centre immediately!"

*

"Attack them! Attack them now!" Commanded George to the Hydra and Griffin. At first the two creatures did not respond, then slowly they began to move towards the girls. Cautiously Anne and Lucy held hands and slowly backed away from the creatures. At the same time Anne whispered under her breath to her sister, "Make sure George does not realise that we have placed the pistol under the power module. He must not defuse it. We have to stop Sekmet's plans."

She paused for a second, gulped and added out loud what they were both thinking. "Even if it means we die in the explosion as well!"

Lucy nodded in agreement and whispered back. "Our only hope is to appeal to George and see if we can break the hypnotic control that he is under."

Both girls had immediately noticed that George's head was larger than normal and had a strange metallic head band which was controlling him. He was also several inches taller than normal. They guessed that he had undergone similar treatment to that which had turned them blue and green. Hades had enhanced the boy's special abilities as well.

Meanwhile George had become frustrated by how slowly the Hydra and Griffin were closing in on the two girls. He had expected his mind control orders to be obeyed instantly! "What are you creatures waiting for? Get those girls!"

Even more frustrating for him, this time the girls did not back away. Instead they calmly let go of each other's hands and walked to opposite sides of the Command Centre.

Lucy spoke first, forcing her voice to sound calm and controlled. "George, your two creatures are hesitating. That is because they do not want to attack us."

Angrily the boy turned to face her but before he could respond to her taunt, Anne interrupted from the other direction. "Do you know why they do not want to attack us?"

Forcing her voice to sound strong and assertive, Anne did not give him a chance to respond. "It is because they are controlled by you. They are connected to your mind and can feel your emotions. And they sense that you do not really want to harm us."

"Rubbish!" responded George angrily, his eyes blinking wildly.

"It's true!" interrupted Lucy, deliberately distracting him again from the other direction. "And because you are our brother you do not want to harm us. At the back of your mind you know that you do not want to hurt us. And because of that your two monsters will not attack us."

"I do not have a family!" he responded. "Hades is my only friend!"

"No, we are your sisters!" interrupted Anne.

George stood silent for a moment as if suddenly confused and dazed. Then his head began to twitch uncontrollably. This gave Anne the opportunity to press home her emotional attack. Now she was certain that they were succeeding in penetrating the mind control he was under. She could see the metal head band starting to glow and make buzzing sounds.

"Believe us George. Despite your hypnosis and brainwashing, somewhere at the back of your mind you still remember us. You still remember and love your family."

The boy closed his eyes and shook his head as if trying to clear it of confusion. Meanwhile the Hydra and Griffin stopped and sat down, like pet dogs waiting for instructions from their master.

Next Lucy spoke, deliberately distracting the boy back towards her, hoping to increase his confusion and break the brainwashing. "You are our brother and we love you. That is why we came searching for you, to rescue you from your captors."

In response the boy began to shake all over, his arms twitching uncontrollably. Suddenly George fell to his knees and held his head in both hands. It was all he could do to hold back his tears. Then with a scream of anger he yanked the metallic head band off and threw it away. Sparks immediately spat from where it had been connected to his head. Then with a loud yell he pulled out the remaining wires from the skin on his temples.

"I remember. I remember. It's all coming back to me. I remember everything!"

Immediately his sisters ran forward and tried to help him to his feet. Was he free from his brainwashing?

*

The princess sped down the main corridor as fast as she could, carrying a long barrelled shock rifle which she had got from the armoury en-route.

Not far behind ran Hades, his little legs trying to match her fast pace.

"Keep up man! We must get to the Command Centre before they can do any damage."

As she shouted, they rounded the corner and came to the open entrance. Stopping outside she motioned Hades to be silent, then cautiously looked into the Command

Centre. Inside she saw George standing with his two sisters, all hugging and comforting each other. And to her horror she also saw that the Griffin and Hydra were sitting tamely to one side just watching. Sekmet immediately realised what had happened and knew that she had to regain mind control of George as soon as possible. The longer he was free the more difficult it would be to get him back under control! Without hesitation she charged inside, followed by Hades.

Hearing her and Hades entering the Command Centre from behind him, George spun around to face them. "Attack them!" he shouted and pointed at the man and woman. In response, the Hydra and Griffin immediately sprang into action. "Do as I command. Attack the princess and scientist!"

Sekmet somersaulted backwards to get out of their way, but Hades failed to move in time. Both creatures pounced on him in a co-ordinated attack and slashed and tore at him wildly. His screams echoed horribly around the Command Centre as his own creatures ended his life. Sekmet momentarily reflected on the irony of Hades being eaten alive by his own monstrous creations.

Satisfied that their first victim was slain, the two creatures turned their attention to Sekmet. However the princess knew that she had to act quickly before they pounced on her next. She realised that the rifle she held was not powerful enough to kill a full size Titan but it could slay infant ones. If she could strike it dead centre!

Before they could pounce she raised her weapon and blasted the Griffin dead centre. The beast immediately tumbled backwards, letting out a lion-like roar as it hit the floor. Its wings flapped helplessly against the floor and it struggled to roll over and stand up. Finally it let out a long, loud sigh and ceased to move, its four legs pointing rigidly into the air.

Meanwhile the Hydra had crouched down, preparing to pounce; each of its twisting heads hissing loudly. A bite from any one of them could rip her arm off. But she was a warrior and feared nothing. In one fluid movement Sekmet stepped back, took aim and blasted it directly in the chest. Its heads screamed in agony and it reared backwards then slumped to the floor spread eagled. Each head screeched defiantly for a moment then, one at a time, fell silent. Finally a faint plume of smoke curled up from its scorched chest where she had blasted it and it stopped twitching.

George and his sisters stood with their mouths open, their faces a mixture of horror and surprise. They had been certain the two creatures would easily kill Sekmet as well. Instead she stood triumphant with her weapon pointing at them.

"Stay where you are humans!"

George acted on instinct and ignored his headache. Closing his eyes his mind called out silently for help. Even as Sekmet slowly walked up to the startled trio, there was the sound of crashing and banging from the Containment Chamber next door. Holding her gun ready she turned and looked in the direction of the noise, as the inner door burst open and crashed to the floor with a loud clang. Moments later three infant Cyclops staggered through the entrance. Each was about six feet tall. Instantly Sekmet and George both realised that his mental cry for help had brought them to life. Even though he no longer wore the head band and his head was already shrinking back to its normal size, he still had some of his enhanced telepathic power remaining! But even though he had summoned the Cyclops, he realised that whoever gave the creatures their first command, would have total control of them.

Before he could act, the princess pointed at the children and commanded the Cyclops. "Kill the three children!" Immediately the three Cyclops stopped staggering around like confused zombies and turned towards them.

"Attack the children!" ordered Sekmet again loudly. This time the three creatures purposely strode towards them, their arms outstretched, preparing to grab and slash!

Chapter Twenty-Six

Bridgid raced through the underground base as fast as she could, aware that there was only a few minutes left before her bombs detonated. Thankfully the hand held tracking device which she carried was guiding her by the shortest route to the Command Centre. Knowing that Cronus had alerted Hades of her escape, Bridgid had changed plans and was heading to the Command Centre to save the two girls.

After all they had been through, with so little time left, she wondered if they would all perish down here after all.

A moment later she rounded the corner and ran directly through the open door into the Command Centre. In an instant she saw Sekmet and the three Cyclops closing in to attack Anne, Lucy and George. Without hesitation she launched herself across the room and crashed into Sekmet from behind, grabbing hold of her tightly with both arms. They both collapsed onto the floor hard, but Sekmet took most of the impact and lay stunned, while Bridgid was able to scramble to her feet.

"Anne, Lucy and George, escape while you can! I am going to detonate the pistol which you have hidden here."

Anne silently realised what Bridgid intended to do and simply nodded back at her tearfully. Then she grabbed Lucy and George by the hands and fled from the room. Still following Sekmet's original order, the three Cyclops turned and chased after them.

Anne had only just reached the end of the corridor when a loud explosion rocked the floor. The trio were knocked off their feet by the shock wave of the explosion. Behind them smoke and flame billowed out of the Command Centre and filled the corridor. Anne got up first and looked back hoping that the blast had killed the Cyclops. To her horror she saw the three creatures emerge through the swirling smoke, striding after them like pre-programmed robots. Programmed to get Anne, Lucy and George.

Spurred into action Anne pulled her sister and brother sharply to their feet. "Come on you two. We need to get to Sekmet's spacecraft and escape before the entire Hollow Earth blows to bits!"

*

The chamber containing the Titans became noisier and noisier as more and more of the giant tubes began to automatically revive the monsters inside. Then the bottoms of the tubes started to swing open and streams of green liquid slopped onto the floor. Elsewhere in the chamber the time bombs were about to detonate.

In the adjoining chambers the automated moles began to spark into life in preparation for tunnelling into the rock ceilings.

*

Anne dragged her brother and sister through the maze of metal corridors, their feet clanging loudly on the shiny floor. Their frantic, heaving breaths echoed off the walls and ceilings making it sound as if there were dozens of fleeing people. Anne's heart pounded so hard that it felt as if it would burst from her chest. Abruptly the other two staggered to a halt and pulled her back. Reluctantly she too stopped for a moment to catch her breath.

"Have we lost the three Cyclops?" gasped George hopefully.

Lucy looked back down the corridor but could not see them. "It's OK; I think we have lost them at the last bend!"

Anne was not so sure and grabbed them roughly by the arms and dragged them behind her. "Stop talking and keep running; we are almost at the landing area!"

She just hoped that they all had enough energy to keep going for a few more minutes. But even if they reached the spacecraft, how would they fly it? Lucy might have been able to if she still had her enhanced mind; but now she was normal again she would not be able to do it. And George would not be able to either, now he was no longer under Hades hypnotic control.

A moment later she breathed a sigh of relief as they rounded a corner and came to the intersection of three corridors at the entrance to the landing area. They had made it! Then Anne suddenly stopped them all in their tracks, as two of the Cyclops ran down the corridors ahead of them. In response Anne grabbed Lucy and George and turned to run back along the corridor they had come down. But they froze as they saw the third Cyclops advancing silently up behind them. They were trapped!

*

The time bombs hidden in the Titan's chamber began to explode in a sequence of deafening booms. The massive tubes containing the Giants and Titans suddenly shattered, scattering glass fragments and green liquid in all directions. Great jets of goo squirted across the chamber hitting the walls and ceiling. The flammable liquid burst into flames and filled the chamber with swirling layers of fire and poisonous gas. Several of the giant mechanical moles, which were by now upright and had started digging into the chamber's roof; wobbled and fell back to the floor, dislodging large chunks of rock which struck more of the unbroken tubes.

Finally an enormous explosion collapsed the entire chamber's roof, forcing the inferno to shoot along all the corridors, destroying anything in their path.

*

The three Cyclops began to slowly close in on the trapped trio of children, their finger talons flexing menacingly. Their bestial brains were focused on just one thing: stopping the three humans escaping.

Despite being afraid, Anne put herself in front of her brother and sister, trying to shield them from the anticipated attack. Then out of the corner of her mouth she whispered a desperate question to George. "Can you use your mind control on them?"

"I don't think so...but I will try!"

By now his head had returned to normal and he had pulled out the last of the thin wires. Closing his eyes he concentrated for a moment and tried to recall how he was able to control the first creatures Hades had tested him on. For a moment his mind was filled with fear and confusion and then at last he sensed contact with another mind. For a few seconds he had partial control over something and he gambled that it was one of the creatures. In that split second he mentally ordered it to stop before he lost contact. Opening one eye he saw that the middle Cyclops had indeed stopped and the other two were hesitating in their advance towards them. Their single-eyes had glazed over.

"I don't have enough power to turn them away. But I can stop them for a few seconds!" he whispered back to Anne.

"Then what do we do?" gasped Lucy.

In response Anne took a deep swallow and pulled Lucy and George closer to her, fearing the creatures were about to start their attack again. She had no idea what to do next.

The moment she turned her head away from the anticipated attack there was a blinding flash. Out of the corner of her eye she saw that the middle Cyclops was engulfed in a ball of lightening. Amazed, she stared wide-eyed as she saw the creature slump to the floor knocked out cold. It was then that she saw Bridged standing behind the other two creatures, holding Sekmet's long barrelled shock rifle.

Before the remaining Cyclops could turn and attack her, she blasted them both with electrical bolts. Surrounded by swirling electricity they both fell backwards onto the floor out cold. Anne stood wide eyed and open mouthed looking at Bridgid. "We thought you were dead. How did you survive the explosion?"

Bridgid double checked that all the Cyclops were unconscious, then looked up and answered. "The personal force field device I was carrying protected me from the flames of the explosion. The impact of the blast pushed me out through the door and away from the worst of the destruction! Unfortunately I was wounded in the blast, but not enough to stop me using the tracker to find you three." The out-of-breath woman held up her left arm and Anne saw that her suit was torn and her skin beneath badly burned.

Bridgid pointed at the door to the landing area and ordered the trio to follow her. "If we can get to Sekmet's craft in time, I can still fly us out of here!"

As if to reinforce the urgency of the situation, they suddenly felt the heat of the approaching fire as it spread along the corridors towards them. The entire base was on fire. Then as if to reinforce the desperation of their situation, they suddenly felt the first shudder of an earthquake starting beneath them.

Chapter Twenty-Seven

The fire spread rapidly through the base. The inferno from the Titan's chamber, merged with the inferno from the Giant's chamber and surged into the blazing Command Centre. Outside the main base and its corridors, the pipes holding the lava suddenly erupted and spewed the contents out into the maze of rock cut tunnels. Elsewhere massive chunks of the cavern roof collapsed into the river Styx causing a tidal wave. This forced water to surge along the other tunnels throughout the Hollow Earth. Where the freezing water met the white hot lava coming from the other direction; the clash of temperatures caused the rock to crack, triggering a mega-earthquake. In minutes the entire Hollow Earth was shaking and collapsing.

*

Anne and the others scrambled aboard Sekmet's spacecraft and made their way to the control bridge. Bridgid was first to reach the controls and immediately started to activate the flight instruments. "Strap yourselves in; this is going to be a bumpy ride!"

As Anne secured herself into a flight chair she marvelled at how easily Bridgid was able to bring the craft's controls to life. As if reading her thoughts, the woman turned and looked back at Anne. "I have Sekmet's wrist control and know that she has not changed any of the access codes. This time none of the Hollow Earth's defences will attack us as we escape.

Also this craft's force field will allow us to get safely through the lava field on the surface."

Finally she looked to make certain that the three youngsters were all strapped in and then turned back and activated the launch controls. The speed of the acceleration forced them all back into their chairs and for a moment it knocked the air from their lungs. Anne's head spun as the craft twisted and turned its way up through the tunnel system to the surface; avoiding routes that had collapsed or were blocked with lava. She also heard noises coming from outside the craft. The noise caused by the network of air locks, power stations and tunnels exploding behind them. Even worse, ahead of them she could see whole chunks of the shaft's ceiling collapsing.

Skilfully Bridgid teased the controls and zigzagged the craft between the falling columns of rock. Then finally the craft tilted and began to fly vertically on its final ascent to the lava fields in Mount Erebus. Anne gripped the chair tightly as they rushed vertically upwards through all the security defences. Behind them a jet of fire surged up the shaft after them.

*

The freezing cold of Antarctica was shattered as the top of the ice covered volcano exploded. Jets of smoke, flame and fiery rocks blasted miles into the clear blue sky and among them was the singed but undamaged spacecraft.

*

The craft slowly descended vertically into the woods close to Anne's home, scattering dust, leaves and twigs from the ground. Apart from that slight disturbance, Bridgid had succeeded in maintaining the craft's stealth mode throughout the flight home.

It was starting to get dark as the evening arrived and stars began to appear. "Back home just in time," said Lucy with a loud sigh of relief.

"Our parents will just think we have been at school all day and stayed on at an after school club," added George gleefully.

Anne nodded quietly in agreement but had more serious thoughts racing through her head. "The three of us are back to normal, no more special powers. Therefore we have to keep all of this adventure a secret. Firstly because no one will believe us and secondly because if they do, then some sinister government agency will probably want to experiment on us!"

All three were back in their school clothes, as Bridgid had been able to re-form their molecules from the craft's memory banks.

Bridgid nodded as well and despite her injured arm, she hugged them all one at a time. With sadness Anne realised that it was a farewell hug. "What will you do now Bridgid. Where will you go?"

The woman began to study the craft's controls again and responded to the question without turning around to face Anne. "I have to leave Earth because humans must not get hold of this craft's technology. It would be too dangerous. Instead I will return to my planet and report that my mission is complete. However I suspect that some of the Titans may have survived the explosions and are still trapped in what remains of the Hollow Earth."

George looked worried."Will they get out?"

Realising that she should not have suggested that, Bridgid tried to calm his fears. "I doubt it, now that all the mechanical moles have been destroyed." As she spoke she continued to work on the navigation controls, plotting a route back to her home planet. However Anne came up to her, eager to ask one last question.

"What happened to the twelve Zodiac Crystals that were hidden across time by Jaxar and Dinvad ten thousand years ago?"

Bridgid turned to face the three humans and smiled; happy to give such important information to people who had proved themselves brave and trustworthy.

"A few years ago a human school boy called James Lightwater; who was a descendent of the survivors of Atlantis, created a fossil finder device. He located special rocks which contained time travel gas. This enabled him to create a time travel suit. With the help of others he went on a dangerous quest to get all the crystals. He succeeded and used their combined power to stop an alien takeover of the Earth. No one else knows about it because his family managed to keep it a secret. Having saved the world he vanished, taking the crystals with him.

No one knows where he went, not even us. Although we thought he might be trying to reach us on our home planet to make contact with us and discover what happened to the other survivors of Atlantis. Who knows, perhaps he will return to Earth again if it is in danger?"

Anne frowned. "What about his family left here on Earth?"

Bridgid thought for a moment. "His sister also inherited crystal-user powers like he has, but as there are no Zodiac Crystals on Earth she has no power. Who knows, perhaps you three are also potential crystal users!"

Bridgid bid them farewell one last time and then teleported them out of the Control Bridge and into the woods outside.

Facing the craft, the trio waved goodbye as it rose vertically into the darkening sky, its silent engines only causing a brief wash of cool air around them.

"It's all over..." said Lucy feeling half glad and yet half sad. However she was secretly concerned that they might still have some residue special powers in their bodies which could re-emerge at any time.

George nodded, but still worried about how easily his mind had been taken over and whether someone else might get control of him in the future.

Anne pondered for a moment, looking up at the stars. "I have a strange feeling that we might meet this James Lightwater and his crystals sometime in the future"

The End?

Lightning Source UK Ltd.
Milton Keynes UK
UKOW06f0408310316

271231UK00009B/138/P